She pulled a handkerchief out of her pocket, blew her nose vigorously, and then she smiled at him.

A big, wide smile that completely altered her face, making it soft and luminous, almost pretty, and he found himself smiling back. And as he continued to stare at her, he suddenly realised something else. He wanted to reach out, gather her into his arms, and tell her he'd make everything all right—and that was *insane*.

What on earth was happening to him? he wondered. He didn't 'do' protective, any more than he 'did' apologies, and just because she was sitting there looking so tiny, her lips parted in a wide smile…

Feeling protective of a woman was right up there alongside involvement, commitment, on the list of things he'd spent a lifetime avoiding.

'Eli?'

Uncertainty was slowly replacing the gratitude in her eyes, and he shook his head to clear it.

'Well, I owe you one for Peg, don't I?' he said, and saw her smile disappear and hurt replace it.

'I wouldn't have told anyone about her,' she said, her voice low, subdued.

He knew she wouldn't, but somehow he had to distance himself from this woman, because he could feel an abyss opening up in front of him. A yawning abyss which would be oh, so easy to fall into.

When a caller's voice echoed over the airwaves he grabbed the receiver like a lifeline.

Maggie Kingsley says she can't remember a time when she didn't want to be a writer, but she put her dream on hold and decided to 'be sensible' and become a teacher instead. Five years at the chalk face was enough to convince her she wasn't cut out for it, and she 'escaped' to work for a major charity. Unfortunately—or fortunately!—a back injury ended her career, and when she and her family moved to a remote cottage in the north of Scotland it was her family who nagged her into attempting to make her dream a reality. Combining a love of romantic fiction with a knowledge of medicine gleaned from the many professionals in her family, Maggie says she can't now imagine ever being able to have so much fun legally doing anything else!

Recent titles by the same author:

A BABY FOR EVE
A WIFE WORTH WAITING FOR
THE CONSULTANT'S ITALIAN KNIGHT
A CONSULTANT CLAIMS HIS BRIDE

A NURSE
TO TAME
THE PLAYBOY

BY
MAGGIE KINGSLEY

First published in Great Britain 2010
Harlequin Mills & Boon Limited,
Eton House, 18-24 Paradise Road, Richmond, Surrey TW9 1SR

© Maggie Kingsley 2010

ISBN: 978 0 263 21513 7

For my father,
who was always my severest critic,
and who I very much hope would have enjoyed this book.

CHAPTER ONE

Monday, 10:05 p.m.

IT WAS a truism known to every woman over the age of twen-ty-five, Brontë O'Brian thought wryly as she gazed down through the large observation window at the man standing below her in the forecourt of ED7 ambulance station. There were two types of men in the world. There were the depend-able men, the reliable men, the men who—if you had any sense—you settled down with, and then there were men like Elijah Munroe.

'He's quite something, isn't he?' Marcie Gallagher, one of the callers from the Emergency Medical Dispatch Centre, observed wistfully as she joined her.

'So I've heard,' Brontë replied.

And not just heard. She knew exactly how tall Elijah Munroe was—six feet two—how his thick black hair flopped so endearingly over his forehead, how his startlingly blue eyes could melt ice, and how his smile always started at one corner of his mouth, then spread slowly across his face, until every woman—be she nineteen or ninety—was lost.

'Unfortunately, Eli doesn't do long term,' Marcie contin-ued, and Brontë nodded.

She knew that, too. She knew that for a couple of months every woman Elijah dated walked around on air, completely convinced he was The One, until one morning with a smile—always with that smile—he was gone.

'I'm surprised one of his ex-girlfriends hasn't skewered him with a surgical instrument,' she observed, and Marcie shrugged.

'What reason could you give? It's not like he promises he'll stay. He's always upfront about not being into commitment.'

'Very clever.'

'Honest, surely?' Marcie protested.

No, clever, Brontë thought firmly, as she noticed that Elijah Munroe had been joined by the head of ED7 ambulance station, George Leslie. Very clever indeed to always be able to get exactly what he wanted by appearing to be upfront and on the level, but then she'd never thought Elijah was a stupid man.

'Only a leopard who never changes his spots,' she muttered under her breath, but Marcie heard her.

'You know him?' she said, curiosity instantly plain on her lovely face, and Brontë shook her head quickly.

Which wasn't a lie. Not a complete lie. Elijah having dated three of her ex-flatmates before just as quickly dumping them hardly qualified as knowing him, especially as the one time they'd met in Wendy's hallway he'd walked straight past her without a word. A fact which still rankled considerably more than it should have done.

'We're all eaten up with curiosity, wondering who he's been dating for the past couple of months,' Marcie continued. 'Normally we find out within twenty-four hours, but he's been remarkably coy about his current girlfriend.'

Coy wasn't a word Brontë would have used to describe Elijah Munroe. Rat fink, low-life, scumbag… Those were the words she would have used but she had no intention of telling Marcie Gallagher that.

'It's quarter past ten,' she said instead. 'I'd better get down to the bay.'

'Can you find your own way there?' Marcie asked. 'I'd take you myself, but…'

'You need to get back to EMDC for the start of your shift.' Brontë smiled. 'No problem.'

And Elijah Munroe wouldn't be a problem either, she told herself as Marcie Gallagher hurried away. So what if she was going to be shadowing him around the Edinburgh streets for the next seven nights, watching his every move? She was thirty-five years old, knew exactly how he operated, how many hearts he'd broken, and that knowledge gave her power.

Oh, who was she kidding? she thought as she turned back to the observation window in time to see Elijah smile at something George Leslie had said and felt her heart give a tiny wobble. Knowing his reputation didn't make her any less susceptible to his charm, and he had charm by the bucket load.

'Which means it's just as well Elijah Munroe only ever dates pretty women,' she told her reflection in the glass. 'Pretty women with model-girl figures, and impossibly long legs, and you don't fit the bill on any of those counts.'

For which she was truly grateful. Or at least she should try to be, she thought with a sigh as she squared her shoulders and walked towards the staircase which would lead her down to the very last man on earth she had ever wanted to work with.

'Why me?'

Elijah Munroe's tone was calm, neutral, and if George Leslie hadn't been his boss for five years he might have been deceived, but George wasn't deceived.

'I don't suppose you'd settle for, "Why not you?"' he said with a broad, avuncular smile, then sighed as Elijah gave him a hard stare. 'No, I didn't think you would. Eli, we both know Frank's going to be off sick for at least a fortnight. I've no one to team you up with, and I can't send out an ambulance unless it's two-manned, so unless you'd rather sit on your butt in the office…'

'I'm stuck with the number cruncher,' Eli finished for him. 'You do realise sending her out on the road with me is probably illegal? Okay, so she's only going to drive, but what if I discover I need help—that I've been sent on a two-man job?'

'Miss O'Brian is a fully qualified nurse. In fact, she was a charge nurse in A and E at the Waverley General until a year ago,' George Leslie declared triumphantly, and Eli frowned.

ED7 ambulance station might be situated in the heart of Edinburgh's old town, which meant most of the patients he collected ended up in the Pentland Infirmary, but he'd occasionally had to go to the Waverley and he couldn't remember any nurse called O'Brian.

'George—'

'Eli, if the ambulance service have decided she's not just qualified enough to drive, but also to assist you if required, that's good enough for me, and it should be good enough for you.'

'Yes, but—'

'Seven nights,' George Leslie said in his best placating tone. 'Seven night shifts when she'll drive you around—'

'Noting down all she considers to be ED7's inefficiencies—'

'Which is why it's vital you keep her sweet,' George Leslie declared, then his lips twitched. 'And I know how easy it is for you to keep women sweet.'

'Anyone ever tell you you'd make an excellent pimp?' Eli said drily, and his boss's smile widened.

'Oh, come on, Eli, it's common knowledge you've a way with the ladies.'

'And right now I'm on the wagon. And before you ask,' Eli continued as his boss's eyebrows rose, 'it's not because I've contracted a sexually communicable disease. I've just decided to take a break from dating for three months.'

'Eli, I'm not asking you to get inside Miss O'Brian's knickers,' George protested. 'Just to be as pleasant and as winning as I know you can be with women. Look, there's a lot riding on this government report,' he continued swiftly as Eli opened his mouth clearly intending to argue. 'There's talk of amalgamating stations, job cuts—'

'But we're already pared right back to the bone,' Eli declared angrily, and his boss nodded.

'Exactly, but in the current economic situation the authorities are looking for ways to save money, and if they can shut down a station they will.'

'But—'

George Leslie put out his hand warningly.

'Miss O'Brian's just arrived,' he said in an undertone. 'I'll leave you to introduce yourself, but you be nice to her, okay? There's a hell of a lot riding on her report.'

Which was great, just great, Eli thought as his boss hurried away. He didn't want to be 'nice', he didn't want to be the poster boy for the station. All he wanted was for this number cruncher to go away and annoy the hell out of someone else but, dutifully, he pasted a smile to his face and turned to face the woman he was going to be sharing his ambulance with for the next seven nights.

At least she wasn't a looker, he decided as he watched her walk towards him. Having managed to stick to his 'no dating' decision for the past two months, it would have been plum awkward if she'd turned out to be a looker, but she was… ordinary. Mid-thirties, he guessed, which was younger than he'd been expecting, scarcely five feet tall, with short brown hair styled into a pixie cut, a pair of clear grey eyes, and her figure… He tilted his head slightly, but it was impossible to tell whether she was buxom or slender when she was wearing the regulation green paramedic cargo trousers, and bulky high-visibility jacket which concealed pretty much everything.

'Thirty-six, twenty-six, and none of your business.'

His head jerked up. 'Sorry?'

'My measurements,' she replied. 'You were clearly scoping me out, so I thought I'd save you the trouble.'

Not ordinary after all, he thought, seeing a very definite hint of challenge in her grey eyes. Sassy. He liked sassy. Sassy was always a challenge and, where women were concerned, he liked a challenge.

No, he didn't, he reminded himself. No dating, no involvement for one more month. He'd made the three-month pledge, he intended to stick to it, and yet, despite himself, a lifetime of pleasing women kicked automatically into place, and he upped his smile a notch.

'You haven't,' he observed. 'Saved me the trouble, that is,' he added as her eyebrows rose questioningly. 'There's still the unanswered question of, "none of your business."'

'Interesting approach,' she said coolly. 'Do the staff at this station always assess the physical attributes of government assessors?'

'Only the pretty ones,' he replied, upping his smile to maximum, but to his surprise she didn't blush, or look even remotely confused, as most women did when he complimented them.

Instead, she held up three fingers and promptly counted them off.

'Number one, I'm not pretty. Number two, charm offensives don't work on me so save your breath and, number three, I'm here to assess the efficiency of this station so your personal opinion of my looks is completely irrelevant.'

Uh-huh, he thought, wincing slightly. So, Miss O'Brian

was no pushover. That would teach him to make assumptions, and it was something he wouldn't do again.

'I think we should restart this conversation,' he said, holding out his hand and rearranging his smile into what he hoped was a suitably contrite one. 'I'm Elijah Munroe. My friends call me Eli, and I'm very pleased to meet you.'

'I'm Miss O'Brian, and I'll let you know in due course whether I can reciprocate the pleasure,' she replied, shaking his hand briefly, then releasing it just as fast.

Snippy, as well as sassy. Well, two could play that game, he decided.

'No problem,' he observed smoothly, 'but though I fully understand your desire to keep our relationship strictly professional, I feel I should point out that calling you by your full name could prove a little time-consuming in an emergency.'

And that is round three to me, sweetheart, he thought with satisfaction, seeing a faint wash of colour appear on her cheeks.

'Fair point,' she conceded, and then, with clear and obvious reluctance, she said, 'My name is Brontë. Brontë O'Brian.'

A faint bell rang somewhere in the deepest recesses of his mind, but he couldn't for the life of him quite grasp it.

'Brontë. Brontë…' he repeated with a frown. 'Could we possibly have met before? Your Christian name… It sounds strangely familiar.'

Damn, damn, and damn, Brontë thought irritably. Why couldn't her parents have called her something completely forgettable, like Mary, or Jane? If they'd given her an 'ordinary' first name she would have remained as forgettable as she'd obviously been that night in Wendy's hallway, and she most certainly didn't want to jog his memory.

'It probably sounds familiar because of the Brontë sisters,' she said quickly. 'As in Charlotte—'

'Emily, and Anne,' he finished for her, then grinned as

she blinked. 'And there was you thinking the only books I would read would be ones with big, colourful pictures, and three words across the bottom of every page.'

It was so exactly what she'd been thinking that she could feel her cheeks darkening still further, but no way was she going to let him get away with it.

'Of course I didn't,' she lied. 'I just didn't take you for a fan of Victorian literature.'

'Ah, but you see that's where a lot of people make a mistake,' he observed. 'Taking me solely at face value.'

And it was a mistake she wouldn't make again, she decided. He might still be smiling at her, but all trace of warmth had gone from his blue eyes, and a shiver ran down her back which had nothing to do with the icy November wind blowing across the open forecourt.

'Which of these vehicles is our ambulance?' she asked, deliberately changing the subject, but, when he pointed to the one they were standing beside, her mouth fell open. 'But that's…'

'Ancient—clapped out—dilapidated.' He nodded. 'Yup.'

'But…' She shook her head. 'I don't understand. The ambulance I passed my LGV C1 driving test on… It was state of the art, with a hydraulic lift—'

'We had seven of those,' he interrupted. 'Unfortunately, five are currently off the road because the hydraulic tail-lifts keep jamming and, believe me, the last thing you want on a wet and windy night in Edinburgh is your patient stuck halfway in, and halfway out, of your ambulance.'

'Right,' she said faintly, and saw his lips twist into a cynical smile.

'Welcome to the realities of the ambulance service, Brontë.'

Welcome indeed, she thought, but she point-blank refused to believe all those ambulances could have been faulty. She'd read the documentation, the glowing reports. Not once had the hydraulic system failed on the ambulance she had been given to prepare her for her driving test, which meant either ED7 had received five faulty vehicles—which she didn't think was likely—or the crews were running them into the ground.

'Top left, breast pocket.'

'Sorry?' she said in confusion, and he pointed at her chest.

'Your notebook—the notebook you're just itching to get out to report this station for trashing their ambulances—it's in your top left, breast pocket. Your pen is, too.'

Damn, he was smart. Too smart.

'Can I take a look round your cab?' she said tightly. 'As I'm going to be driving you, I'd like to see if the layout is any different to what I passed my test on.'

'Be my guest,' he said, but, as she put one foot inside the driver's door, she saw him frown. 'You'll need to change those boots.'

'Why?' she protested, following his gaze down to her feet. 'I'm wearing regulation, as supplied, boots.'

'And they're rubbish. None of us wear government-issue boots. These boots,' he continued, pointing at his own feet, 'have stepped in stuff you wouldn't even want to think about, had drunks vomit all over them, been run over by trolleys and, on one memorable occasion, my driver accidentally reversed over my feet, and the boots—and my feet—survived. Take a tip. Buy yourself some boots from Harper & Stolins in Cockburn Street. Their Safari brand is the best.'

'I'll bear that in mind,' she replied, but she wouldn't.

What she *would* do, however, was make a note of the fact that none of the paramedics at ED7 were obeying health and safety rules if they were all refusing to wear the boots they had been issued with.

'Your notebook and pen are still in the same pocket,' he

said with a grin which annoyed the hell out of her. 'Want to note that down, too, while it's fresh in your mind?'

What she wanted to say was, *And how would you like my pen shoved straight up your nose?* but she doubted that would be professional. Instead, she clambered into the driving seat of his ambulance, and glanced at the instrument panel.

'I see you have an MDT—a mobile display terminal—to give you details of each job you're sent on?'

'Yup,' he replied, getting into the passenger seat beside her. 'It's a useful bit of kit, when it's working, but it crashes a lot, which is why this baby—' he patted the radio on the dashboard fondly '—is much more important. Just remember to switch it off when you've finished making or receiving a call because it's an open transmitter which means everything you say is broadcast not only to EMDC but also to every ambulance on the station which can be…interesting.'

It could get a lot more interesting if he didn't back off, and back off soon, she thought grimly.

'All your calls come from the Emergency Medical Dispatch Centre at Oxgangs, don't they?' she said, trying and failing to keep the edge out of her voice.

He nodded. 'Seven years ago the powers that be decided to close all the operations rooms, and replace them with one centralised, coordinating organisation.'

'Which makes sense,' she said. 'Why scatter your controllers about Edinburgh when they can all be in one central place, ensuring the ambulance resources are deployed effectively and efficiently while also maintaining the highest standards of patient care.'

'Well done,' he said, his lips curving into what even the most charitable would have described as a patronising smile. 'That must be word for word from the press cuttings.'

'Which doesn't make it any the less true,' she retorted, and saw his patronising smile deepen.

'Unless, of course, you happened to be one of the

unfortunate callers they decided were surplus to requirement,' he observed, and she gritted her teeth until they hurt.

So much for her being worried she would fall for his charm. The only thing worrying her at the moment was how long she was going to be able to remain in his company without slapping him.

'What's our call sign?' she asked, determinedly changing the conversation.

'A38.' He smiled. 'My age, actually.'

'Really?' she said sweetly. 'I would have said you were much younger.' *Like around twelve, given the way you're behaving.* 'According to government guidelines, you should reach a code red patient in eight minutes, an amber patient in fourteen minutes and a code green in just under an hour. How often—on average—would you say you hit that target?'

'How on earth should I know?' he retorted, then bit his lip as though he had suddenly remembered something. 'Look, can we talk frankly? I mean, not as an employee of the ambulance service and an employee of a government body,' he continued, 'but as two ordinary people?'

She was pretty sure there was an unexploded bomb in his question. In fact, she was one hundred per cent certain there was but, having got off to such a bad start, the next seven nights were going to seem like an eternity if they didn't at least try to come to some sort of understanding.

'Okay,' she said.

He let out a huff of air.

'I don't want you in my cab. I don't mean you, as in you personally,' he added as she frowned. 'I don't want *any* time-and-motion expert sitting beside me, noting down a load of old hogwash. There are things wrong with the ambulance service—we all know that—but what it needs can't be fixed by number crunching. We need more money, more personnel, and more awareness from a small—but unfortunately rather active—sector of the public that we're not a glorified taxi service for minor ailments.'

'And what makes you think I'm going to be noting down nothing but a load of old hogwash?' she asked, and heard him give a hollow laugh.

'Because it's what you bureaucratic time-and-motion people *do*, what you're paid for, to compare people and how they perform in given situations, and then find fault with them.'

She opened her mouth to reply, then closed it again, and stared at him indecisively. How honest could she be with him? She supposed he'd been honest with her, so maybe it was time for her to be honest with him. At least up to a point.

'Would it reassure you to know this is the first time I've been sent out on an assessment?' she said. 'I've done all of the training, of course, but you're my first case, so the one thing I can promise is I won't be comparing you to anyone.'

He met her gaze in silence for a full five seconds and then, to her dismay, he suddenly burst out laughing.

'Dear heavens, if it's not bad enough to be stuck with a number cruncher, I have to get stuck with a *rookie* number cruncher!'

'Now, just a minute,' she protested, two spots of angry colour appearing on her cheeks, 'you were the one who said we should be honest with each other, and now you're laughing at me, and it's *not* funny.'

He let out a snort, swallowed deeply, and said in a voice that shook only slightly, 'You're right. Not funny. Definitely not funny.'

'*Thank you,*' she said with feeling, and he nodded, then his lips twitched.

'Actually—when you think about it—you've got to admit it is a *little* bit funny.'

She met his eyes with outrage, and it was her undoing. If the laughter in his eyes had been smug, and patronising, she really would have slapped him, but there was such genuine warmth and amusement in his gaze that a tiny choke of laughter broke from her.

'Did you just laugh?' he said, tilting his head quizzically at her. 'Could I possibly have just heard the smallest chuckle from you?'

Brontë's choke of laughter became a peal. 'Okay, all right,' she conceded, 'it *is* funny, but it's not my fault you're my first victim. Someone has to be, but I promise I won't bring out any manacles or chains.'

'Actually, I think I might rather like that.'

His voice was liquid and warm and, as her eyes met his, she saw something deep and dark flicker there, and a hundred alarm bells went off in her head.

No, Brontë, *no*, she told herself as her heart rate accelerated. Just a moment ago you wanted to hit him, and now he's most definitely flirting with you, and any woman who responds to an invitation to flirt with Elijah Munroe has to be one sandwich short of a picnic.

'Shouldn't…' She moistened her lips and started again. 'Shouldn't we be hitting the road? Our shift started at ten-thirty, and—' she glanced desperately at her watch '—it's already ten-forty.'

'We can certainly go out,' he agreed. 'But, strange as it might seem, we don't normally go looking for patients. Normally we wait for them to phone us, but if you want to go kerb crawling with me…'

Oh, *hell*, she thought, feeling a deep wash of colour stain her cheeks. Of course they had to wait for calls, she knew that, but did he have to keep on looking at her with those sun-kissed, Mediterranean-blue eyes of his? They flustered her, unsettled her, and the last thing she needed to feel in Elijah Munroe's company was flustered so, when the radio on the dashboard crackled into life, she grabbed the receiver gratefully.

'ED7 here,' she declared, only to glance across at Eli, bewildered, when she heard a snicker of feminine laughter in reply. 'What did I do wrong?'

'This station is ED7,' he said gently. 'We're A38, remember?'

Great start, Brontë, she thought, biting her lip. Really tremendous, professional start. Not.

'Sorry,' she muttered. 'A38 here.'

'Pregnant woman,' the disembodied voice declared. 'Laura Thomson, experiencing contractions every twenty minutes. Number 12, Queen Anne's Gate.'

Brontë had the ambulance swinging out of the forecourt and onto the dark city street before the dispatcher had even finished the call.

'Should I hit the siren?' she asked, and Eli shook his head.

'No need. We'll be there in under five minutes despite the roads being frosty but, with contractions so close, I wonder why she's waited so long to call us?'

Brontë wondered the same thing when they arrived at the house to discover the tearful mother-to-be's contractions were coming considerably closer than every twenty minutes.

'I've been trying to get hold of my husband,' Laura Thomson explained. 'He's working nights at the supermarket to earn us some extra money, and this is our first baby, and he's my birthing partner.'

'I'm afraid he's going to miss out on that unless he arrives in the next five minutes,' Eli replied ruefully as the young woman doubled up with a sharp cry of pain. 'In fact, I'd be happier if you were in Maternity right now.'

'But my husband won't know where I am,' the young woman protested. 'He'll come home, and I won't be here, and he'll be so worried.'

Brontë could see the concern on Eli's face, and she felt it, too. A quick examination had revealed Laura Thomson's cervix to be well dilated and, if they didn't go, there was a very strong possibility she was going to have her baby in the ambulance.

Quickly, she picked up a discarded envelope from the table, scrawled, 'Gone to the Pentland Maternity' on it, then placed the envelope on the mantelpiece.

'He'll see that, Laura,' she declared, and the woman nodded, then doubled up again with another cry of pain.

'Okay, no debate, no argument, we go *now*,' Eli declared, and before Brontë, or Laura Thomson, had realised what he was going to do he had swept Laura up into his arms as though she weighed no more than a bag of flour. 'Drive fast, Brontë,' he added over his shoulder as he strode out the door, 'drive *very* fast!'

She didn't get the chance to. She had barely turned the corner at the bottom of Queen Anne's Gate when Eli yelled for her to stop.

'This baby isn't waiting,' he said after she'd parked, then raced round to the back of the ambulance and climbed in. 'How much maternity experience do you have?'

'Not much,' Brontë admitted. 'We didn't tend to get mums-to-be arriving in A and E.'

'Well, welcome to the stork club,' he replied. 'The baby's head is already crowning, and the contractions are coming every minute.'

'I want…my husband,' Laura Thomson gasped. 'I want him here *immediately*.'

'Just concentrate on your breathing,' Eli urged. 'Believe me, you can do this on your own.'

'I know,' Laura exclaimed, turning bright red as she bore down again. 'I just want him here so I can *kill* him because, believe me, if this is what giving birth is like, this baby is never going to have any brothers and sisters!'

A small muscle twitched near the corner of Eli's mouth.

'Okay, when your son or daughter is born, you have my

full permission to kill your husband,' he replied, carefully using his hand to control the rate of escape of the baby's head, 'but right now work with the contractions, don't try to fight against them.'

'That's…easy…for you to say,' Laura said with difficulty. 'And…I…can…tell…you…this. If there is such a thing as reincarnation…' She gritted her teeth and groaned. 'Next time I'm coming back as a man!'

'You and me both, Laura,' Brontë declared, seeing Eli slip the baby's umbilical cord over its head, then gently ease one of its shoulders free, 'but if you could just give one more push I think your son or daughter will be here.'

Laura screwed up her face, turned almost scarlet again and, with a cry that was halfway between a groan and a scream, she bore down hard, and with a slide and a rush the baby shot out into Eli's hands.

'Is it all right?' Laura asked, panic plain in her voice as she tried to lever herself upright. 'Is my baby all right?'

'You have a beautiful baby girl, Laura,' Eli replied, wincing slightly as the baby let out a deafening wail. 'With a singularly good pair of lungs. Are there two arteries present in the cord?' he added under his breath, and Brontë nodded as she clamped it.

'What about the placenta?' she murmured back.

'Hospital. Let's get them both to the hospital,' he replied, wrapping the baby in one of the ambulance's blankets. 'Giving birth in the back of an ambulance isn't ideal, and I'll be a lot happier when both mum and baby are in Maternity.'

Brontë couldn't have agreed more and, by the time they had delivered Laura and her daughter to Maternity, the young mother seemed to have completely forgotten her pledge to kill her husband if her beaming smile when he arrived, looking distinctly harassed, was anything to go by.

'That's one we won tonight,' Eli observed when he and Brontë had returned to the ambulance.

She smiled, and nodded, but his good humour didn't last. Not when they then had several call-outs for patients who could quite easily have gone to their GPs in the morning instead of calling 999. She knew what Eli was thinking as she watched his face grow grimmer and grimmer. That as a government assessor she must be noting down all of these nonemergency calls, would be putting them in her report as proof positive that ED7's services could be cut and, though part of her wanted to reassure him, she knew she couldn't. Assessing, and criticising, was supposed to be what she was here for, but she felt for him, and the depth of her sympathy surprised her.

'Coffee,' Eli announced tightly when he and Brontë strode through the A and E waiting room of the Pentland Infirmary after they'd delivered a city banker who confessed in the ambulance to having twisted his ankle two weeks before, but had been 'too busy' to go to his GP. 'I need a coffee, and I need it now.'

'Sounds good to me,' Brontë agreed, but, as she began walking towards the hospital canteen, she suddenly realised Eli was heading towards the hospital exit. 'I thought you said you wanted a coffee?' she protested when she caught up with him.

'Not here,' he said. 'The coffee they serve here would rot your stomach. Tony's serves the best coffee in Edinburgh, and it's where all the ambulance crews go.'

'But—'

'Look, just drive, will you?' he exclaimed. 'Buccleuch Street, top of The Meadows, you can't miss it.'

Just drive, will you. Well, that was well and truly putting her in her place, she thought angrily, and for a second she debated pointing out that she was a government assessor, not a taxi driver, but she didn't. Instead, she silently drove to Buccleuch Street, but, when she pulled the ambulance up outside a small building with a blinking neon sign which proclaimed it to be Tony's Twenty-four Hours Café, she kept the engine running.

'Eli, what if we get a call?' she said as he jumped down from the cab.

'Hit the horn, and I'll come running. Black coffee, café au lait, latte or cappuccino?'

'Cappuccino, no sugar, lots of chocolate sprinkles, but—'

'Do you want anything to eat?' Eli interrupted.

'No, but—'

'You'll be sorry later,' he continued. 'Tony's makes the best take-away snacks, and meals, in Edinburgh.'

He probably did, she thought, as Eli disappeared into the café. Just as she was equally certain Eli would instantly come running if she had to hit the horn, but did he have to make life so difficult for himself? Of course he was legally entitled to a break, and he could take it wherever he chose, but biting her head off was not a smart move. One word from her and he could be out of a job.

And you're going to say that one word? a little voice whispered in the back of her head, and she blew out a huff of impatience. Of course she wouldn't. She'd felt as frustrated as he had by some of the calls, and from what she'd seen he possessed excellent medical skills. He just also very clearly detested bureaucracy and, to him, she was the living embodiment of that bureaucracy. If only he would meet her halfway. If only he would accept she was finding this as difficult as he was. And if only he hadn't brought a hamburger back along with their two coffees, she thought with dismay when Eli opened the ambulance door and the pungent aroma of fried onions filled the air.

'You're not actually going to eat that, are you?' she said, wrinkling her nose as he got into the passenger seat, and the smell of onions became even stronger.

'You have something against hamburgers?' he replied, taking a bite out of his and swallowing with clear relish.

'Not at the proper time,' she declared, 'but at half past three in the morning…?'

'Well, the way I figure it,' he observed, 'if we worked a nine-to-five job like regular people, this would be lunchtime.'

'Right,' she said without conviction. She took a sip of her coffee, then another. 'Actually, this is very good.'

'Told you Tony's made the best coffee in Edinburgh,' he said, stretching out his long legs and leaning his head back against the headrest. 'And nothing beats a good dose of caffeine on a night when you seem to have picked up so many patients who aren't even code greens.'

She shot him a sideways glance. All too clearly she remembered the instructions she had been given. Don't ever become personally involved with a station you have been sent out to assess. Remain coldly objective, and clinical, at all times.

Oh, blow the instructions, she decided.

'Look, Eli, I can completely understand your frustration with some of the people we've picked up tonight,' she declared, 'but the trouble is, though the vast majority of the population realise, and accept, they should only call 999 in an emergency, there's a very small number who seem to think if they arrive in A and E by ambulance they'll be seen a lot faster even if there's nothing very much wrong with them.'

'Yeah, well, one visit to A and E would soon disabuse them of that,' he replied. 'In my day, if there was any indication that a patient was simply trying to queue jump, we made them wait even longer.'

'You used to work in A and E?' she said, considerably surprised.

Eli finished the last of his hamburger, crumpled the paper which had been surrounding it into a ball and dropped it into the glove compartment.

'Ten years at the Southern General in Glasgow for my sins. I was charge nurse until I packed it in.'

'Why?' she asked curiously. 'Why did you give it up?'

He took a large gulp of his coffee, and shrugged.

'Too much paperwork, too much time spent chasing big-shot consultants who couldn't be bothered to come down to A and E to see a patient.' He glanced across at her, his blue eyes dark in the street lamp's glow. 'I hear you were a charge nurse in A and E at the Waverley before you became a number cruncher. What made you give it up?'

'Much the same reasons,' she said evasively, and his gaze became appraising.

'Nope. There was something else.'

She shifted uncomfortably in her seat. He was right, there was, but she had no intention of confirming it. Her private life was her own.

'Would you settle for, it's none of your business?' she said.

'Not fair,' he protested. 'I gave you a straight answer.'

'No one ever tell you life isn't fair?' she countered, wishing he would just drop the subject. 'Look, my reasons are my own, okay?'

He gazed at her over the rim of his polystyrene coffee cup.

'I'll find out,' he observed. 'I always do.'

'Omnipotent now, are you?' she said, not bothering to hide her irritation, and he grinned.

'Nah. Just good at wheedling stuff out of people. In fact…'

'In fact, what?' she asked as he came to a sudden halt and stared at her as though he wasn't actually seeing her, but something a million miles away. 'Eli—'

'Of *course*!' he exclaimed, slapping the heel of his hand against his forehead with triumph. '*Now* I remember why your name sounded so familiar. Wendy Littleton, sister in Obs and

Gynae at the Pentland. She and I dated a couple of years back, and she shared a flat with someone called Brontë. Don't tell me it was you?'

She sighed inwardly. She supposed she could try to deny it, but how many Brontës were there likely to be in Edinburgh, and what did it matter anyway?

'Yes, that was me,' she said with resignation.

'Talk about a small world,' he declared. 'Wendy Littleton. Gorgeous black hair, and big brown eyes, as I recall.'

'Actually, her hair was brown, and her eyes were blue,' Brontë replied drily.

'Oh. Right,' he muttered. 'But you and I never actually met, though, did we?'

Should she be nice, or should she make him squirm? No contest, she decided.

'Yes, we've met,' she replied. 'Just the once, but I obviously didn't make much of an impression. Neither did Wendy, come to think of it,' she continued, 'considering you dumped her.'

'I didn't dum—'

'Dumped—walked out on—call it whatever you like,' she declared. 'The bottom line is she was so miserable after you left she emigrated to Australia. She actually got married a couple of months ago.'

'Well, that's good news,' he said with clear relief but, having started, Brontë wasn't about to stop.

'Not for me, it wasn't,' she said. 'Wendy's father owned the flat we lived in so when she emigrated he sold it to give her some stake money which left me homeless.'

'Oh.'

'Yes, oh.' She nodded. 'Luckily, I managed to get a room in a flat with one of the Sisters in Men's Surgical at the Pentland. Anna Browning. Name ring any bells?'

To her surprise a dark tide of colour crept up the back of his neck.

'Yes,' he said awkwardly. 'Look, Brontë—'

'Unfortunately, Anna went back to Wales after you dumped her,' Brontë continued determinedly, 'so I had to go flat hunting again. Which was how I met Sue Davey of Paediatrics. She was the one with the gorgeous black hair, and big brown eyes.'

'Okay—all right—so you've roomed with some of my ex-girlfriends!' Eli exclaimed with obvious annoyance. 'Dating is hardly a crime, is it?'

No, but making women fall in love with you, and then leaving them, sure is, she wanted to retort, but before she got a chance to say anything their radio bleeped and Eli reached for the receiver.

'A38,' he all but barked.

'Hey, Eli, don't shoot the messenger,' a female voice protested. 'Code amber. Twenty-six-year-old female, Rose Gordon, apparently unable to walk or talk properly. Number 56, Bank Street. Her family's with her.'

'Possible CVA?' Brontë said, quickly emptying the remains of her coffee into the gutter, and putting the ambulance in gear.

'Maybe, maybe not,' Eli declared, clearly still irritated. 'While those symptoms would certainly suggest a stroke, it's better not to go in with any preconceived idea because we could miss something. Luckily, her family are with her so hopefully we'll be able to get more information.'

They did. Though Mr and Mrs Gordon were clearly very upset, they weren't hysterical.

'She's never been like this before,' Mrs Gordon said, looking quickly across at her husband for confirmation. 'She can't walk, or talk, and—' a small sob escaped from her as she glanced back to her daughter who was slumped motionless in a seat '—she seems so confused. It's almost as though she's drunk, but Rose never drinks.'

'Any underlying medical condition we should know about?'

Eli asked, kneeling down beside the young woman to take her pulse.

'Rose is a type 1 diabetic,' Mr Gordon replied, his face white and drawn, 'but she tests herself regularly, never misses an insulin dose, so I don't think it can be linked to that.'

Brontë exchanged glances with Eli. Actually, there was a very good chance it could be. Rose Gordon's face was pale and clammy, her eyes unfocused, and when a type 1 diabetic's sugar level became very low they could all too quickly develop hypoglycaemia which made them appear confused, and agitated, and unable to speak or stand properly.

'Has she been working under a lot of pressure recently?' Brontë asked as she handed Eli one of their medi-bags. 'Changed her routine at all?'

Mrs Gordon shook her head. 'She's a schoolteacher—has been for the past four years—and the pressure's just the same as it always was. As for her routine... I can't think of anything she's doing she hasn't done before.'

'She's going to the gym now before she comes home,' a small voice observed. 'She said it was good for anger management.'

Eli and Brontë turned to see a young boy of about eight hovering by the door, his eyes wide and fearful, and Mrs Gordon reached out and put a comforting arm around his shoulders.

'This is Rose's brother, Tom,' she said. 'Rose will be all right, sweetheart. These nice people will make her all right.'

She sounded as though she was trying to convince herself as much as her young son, but Brontë's mind was already working overtime and, judging by the speed with which she saw Eli take a blood sample from Rose Gordon, his was, too. Exercise could all too easily affect blood sugar. Particularly if the diabetic hadn't eaten enough beforehand to ensure their blood sugar stayed high.

'1.6 mmols,' Eli murmured, handing the sample to Brontë, and she sucked in her breath sharply.

The normal range for a diabetic was between 4.5 and 12.0 mmols so this was dangerously low, and swiftly she handed him some glucagon.

'What's wrong—what's the matter with Rose?' Mrs Gordon asked, panic plain in her voice, as Eli searched for a vein in her daughter's arm.

'She's hypoglycaemic,' Brontë explained. 'My guess is she's forgotten to take a snack before going to the gym and all the energy she's expended has really leached the sugar from her body. Don't worry,' she continued, seeing the concern on the woman's face, 'she'll be fine. Give her fifteen minutes, and she'll be as good as new.'

That the Gordons didn't believe her was plain, but, within fifteen minutes, Rose was standing upright, albeit a little unsteadily, and able to apologise profusely to everyone. Eli gave her some sugar jelly to raise her blood sugar still further and, when Rose's blood sugar reading reached 4.6 mmols, he asked Mrs Gordon to make her some pasta.

'Rose needs carbohydrate,' he explained. 'What I've administered given her a quick boost, but what she needs now is something to give her slow-burning energy.'

Quickly, Mrs Gordon bustled away to the kitchen, and, after reassuring Rose's father that Rose was unlikely to become hypoglycaemic again if she kept her food intake high before she took any exercise, Brontë followed Eli out to the ambulance with a smile.

'It's nice when you can get someone back to normal in such a short time, isn't it?' she said.

'One of the pluses of the job, that's for sure,' Eli replied.

He didn't look as though it was a plus. In fact, as the night wore on, he became more and more morose and, when they eventually returned to ED7, just as dawn was breaking over Edinburgh, Brontë decided enough was enough.

'Look, Eli,' she said after he had handed in his report and she walked with him across the ambulance forecourt towards the street, 'I may be new to this job, but I worked in A and E for seven years. I know all about the people who could quite easily have gone to their GP instead of the hospital and, believe me, I'm not going to be marking either you, or ED7, down because so many of tonight's calls weren't even code greens.'

'I'm not thinking about the people we picked up tonight,' he said impatiently.

'Then what's with the moodiness?' she demanded. 'I know you don't like number crunchers—'

'It's got nothing to do with your job,' he interrupted. 'It's…' He shook his head. 'Personal.'

Personal? She stopped dead on the pavement outside the station, and gulped. He wanted to talk to her about something *personal*? She didn't think she was ready for 'personal,' not when his deep blue eyes were fixed on her, making her feel warm and tingly all over, but he was waiting for her to answer so she nodded.

'Okay,' she said. 'Spill it.'

'What you were saying earlier about your flatmates… I think you should know I'm taking a break from dating.'

Of all the things she had been expecting him to say, that wasn't it, and she stared at him, bewildered.

'And you're telling me this because…?' she said in confusion, and for a moment he looked a little shame-faced, then a slightly crooked smile appeared on his lips.

'I just thought you should know, in case you were concerned I might hit on you, or were hoping…well…you know.'

She straightened up to her full five feet.

'I was hoping *what*?' she said dangerously.

'Oh, come on, Brontë,' he declared, 'it's common knowledge I like women, and they like me.'

She opened her mouth, closed it again, then shook her head in outraged disbelief. 'So you're saying I... You think that I... Sheesh, when they were handing out modesty, you sure were right at the back of the queue, weren't you?'

'Brontë—'

'Believe it or not, *Mr* Munroe,' she continued furiously. 'Whatever charms you supposedly possess leave me completely cold, and if you had attempted—as you so poetically phrased it—to hit on me, you would have required the immediate services of a dentist. You are not my type. You never were, never will be. And even if you *were* my type,' she could not stop herself from adding, 'I'm taking a break from dating myself.'

'Why?'

Damn, but she'd said too much as she always did when she was angry, but she had no intention of revealing any more, and she swung her tote bag high on her shoulder, only narrowly missing his chin.

'I,' she said, her voice as cold as ice, 'am going home to get some sleep, and you... As far as I'm concerned, you can go take a running jump off Arthur's Seat as long as you're back here this evening to do your job.'

'Brontë, listen—'

She didn't. She turned on her heel, and strode off down the street, because she knew if she didn't she would hit him.

The nerve of the man. The sheer unmitigated gall. Implying she might be interested in him, suggesting she might have difficulty keeping her hands off him.

He's right, though, isn't he? a little voice laughed in her head, and she swore under her breath. No, he wasn't. He was smug, and arrogant, and opinionated.

But he has gorgeous eyes, hasn't he?

He did. He had the kind of eyes to die for, and thick black hair which just screamed out to be touched, and as for his broad shoulders...

Hell, but having to work along side Elijah was like being on a diet in a cake shop. You knew he was bad for you, you knew you would deeply regret it, and yet, despite all of that, you were still tempted.

Which didn't mean she was going to give in to temptation. She only had to work with him for another six nights, and not even she could make a fool of herself in that amount of time. And she had no intention of making a fool of herself. She'd done it far too often in the past, and to even consider it with a man who had a reputation like Elijah Munroe's...

'No way, not ever,' she said out loud to the empty Edinburgh street.

CHAPTER TWO

Tuesday, 10:07 p.m.

'I DON'T care how you do it, or who you have to upset, but I am *not* going out with Brontë O'Brian again!'

'Eli, we went through all this yesterday,' George Leslie protested. 'There *is* no one else I can put her with, and if I pull out one of the other guys just to accommodate you, there will be hell to pay.'

'Why can't she work days?' Eli argued. 'She could work days with Luke. He's a trauma magnet, can't leave the station without falling over multiple pile-ups, and I'm sure that would keep Ms O'Brian's employers happy.'

'I suggested she work days when I first heard she was coming,' his boss replied, 'but her employers were insistent she did nights.'

'And we all know what that means,' Eli said irritably. 'They think the worthy Edinburgh folk will be all tucked up tight in their beds at night, so we'll have minimal call-outs, and they can use that as an excuse to make some of us redundant.'

'That's my guess.' George nodded.

'Charlie Woods,' Eli said. 'He owes me a favour. I'm sure he'd be prepared to swap—'

'Except his wife is due to give birth any day now,' George

interrupted. 'Eli, can't you just live with it? Ye gods, you've already done one night, you only have another six to go.'

'You don't know what she's like,' Eli declared. 'She's pig-headed, opinionated, always thinks she's right—'

'Sounds a bit like you.' George grinned.

'I am *nothing* like her,' Eli snapped. 'George, I want out. There has to be a way for you to get me out of this, or I swear…'

'You'll do what?' his boss demanded with clear exasperation. 'Walk out on me? Throw your career down the toilet? For heaven's sake, man, I am not asking you to bond with her, be her best friend forever. All I'm asking is for you to be civil, pleasant, and do the job you're paid for.'

'But—'

'And can I point out it's not just your job on the line if we get a lousy report,' George continued, his normally placid face bright red. 'It's everyone's job, so get a grip of yourself, a smile on your face, and be *nice*.'

Which was easy for George to say, Eli thought as his boss strode away. He didn't have to work with the damn woman. He didn't have to sit beside an interfering know-it-all who was constantly sticking her nose in where it wasn't wanted, and making snide comments about his dating habits.

And that's what this is all about, isn't it? a small voice whispered in his head. *It's got nothing to do with her as a person. It's because of what she said about her flatmates, implying you were some sort of low-life.*

With a muttered oath he kicked out at one of his ambulance wheels angrily. Hell's teeth, but what right did she have to judge his dating habits? It wasn't as though he had ever deceived anyone. It wasn't as though he had ever lied. He had always been upfront, made it clear he wouldn't be sticking around forever, so what was her problem?

She still had it, he thought, as he heard the sound of slow footsteps crossing the forecourt, and turned to see Brontë walking towards him, her face set and tight. Well, I'm not any happier with the situation than you are, sweetheart, he thought, except…

George was right. No matter what his private feelings were, it wasn't just his neck on the line here. If Brontë O'Brian gave ED7 a damning report, a lot of heads would roll. Heads belonging to people he knew. People who had families, commitments, mortgages, so somehow he had to placate this woman, get her onside, and he squared his chin.

'Brontë, can we talk?' he said when she drew level with him.

'It's a free country,' she replied.

Which wasn't exactly the most encouraging of answers and he gritted his teeth. He didn't 'do' apologies—had never in his life felt the need to apologise for anything he'd done—but he was going to apologise now if it killed him.

'About this morning… What I said…' He gritted his teeth even harder. 'I probably seemed a bit arrogant to you, a bit of a prat.'

'Can't argue with that,' she said, and he clenched his fists until the knuckles gleamed white.

She was enjoying this. He would bet money she was enjoying it, and if it hadn't been for George he would have told her to take a hike.

'What I said this morning,' he continued determinedly, 'I shouldn't have said it.'

'No, you shouldn't.'

'Look, I'm apologising here,' he exclaimed, 'so couldn't you at least give me a break, and meet me halfway?'

She tilted her head thoughtfully to one side.

'You've said you were arrogant, and you've said you were a prat,' she observed, 'but I'm not hearing any apology.'

'Okay, all right,' he snapped. 'I'm *sorry*. I was wrong, okay? I shouldn't have said what I did, and I'm *sorry*.'

For a second she said nothing, then, to his surprise, the corners of her mouth tilted slightly upwards.

'Why do I get the feeling you'd rather have your finger-nails pulled out one by one than apologise to anyone about anything?' she said.

A reluctant answering smile was drawn from him. Damn, she was smart, though not for the world would he ever have said so.

'Can we call a truce and start again?' he said. 'I promise I won't open my big mouth if—'

'I don't refer to your ex-girlfriends,' she finished for him, and he nodded.

'So, do we have a deal?' he asked, holding out his hand.

Oh, shoot, she thought, as she took his hand and felt a jolt of electricity run right up her arm. She'd come into work to-night still angry with him, still furious, and yet now she was all too aware that a lean, muscular, highly desirable man was holding her hand, and it felt so good, much too good. How had he done that? How had he managed to turn her emotions upside down in an instant?

Practice, Brontë. Years and years of practice, so watch your step, or you'll end up like all the other girls he's dumped.

'You're frowning at me,' Eli continued, irritation replacing the smile on his face. 'Does that mean you're planning on making me apologise some more, or…?'

'We have a deal,' she agreed, releasing his hand quickly. 'Except…'

His dark eyebrows snapped together. 'Except what?'

'Can I ask you something?' she replied. 'You don't have to answer if you don't want to,' she added quickly as his eyebrows lowered still further, 'but do you ever plan on settling down with just one woman?'

'Heck, no,' he replied. 'I've never been married, or engaged, and I don't intend to be. No ties, no responsibilities, that's my idea of perfection.'

'Sounds to me like someone hurt you pretty badly at some point,' she observed, and he rolled his eyes impatiently.

'Why does there have to be some deep-seated psychological reason for the fact I don't want to be tied down, trapped?'

'There doesn't, I suppose,' she replied, 'but I'm just curious as to what makes a serial dater like you tick.'

One corner of his mouth turned up. 'Sex.'

'And that's it?' she protested.

He grinned. 'Pretty much.'

It was her turn to roll her eyes. 'You're impossible.'

'Look, what you call "serial dating," I call *fun*,' he declared. 'If more people would only realise—accept—nothing lasts, and you should just enjoy the moment, the happier everyone would be.'

Her grey eyes searched his face curiously. 'And are you happy?'

Of all the dumb questions she could have asked, that had to be the dumbest, he decided.

'Of course I'm happy,' he declared. 'I have a job I love, a nice flat, a good circle of friends—why wouldn't I be happy?'

'I'm pleased for you. No, I *mean it*,' she added as he raised a right eyebrow, clearly challenging her remark. 'To be content with your life, to want nothing more, feel you need nothing more... You're very lucky.'

It wasn't luck, he thought, as they both heard their MDT bleep, and Brontë hurried to read the message. It was being realistic, seeing the world for what it was. And he hadn't been lying when he'd said he was happy. Of course he was happy. Okay, so his three months' self-imposed celibacy was beginning to irk big time, and his flat felt empty, lonely, with just himself rattling around it, but the celibacy had been essential after what happened with Zoe. That was a mistake he most definitely didn't want to make again.

'Middle-aged man collapsed in supermarket,' Brontë

announced. 'Seems to be unconscious, no family with him, but the supermarket first-aider is in attendance.'

'Could be anything,' Eli replied. 'Heart attack, drunk, or faker.'

The first-aider clearly didn't think the middle-aged man was faking. She was flapping around in panic when they arrived, and her relief at seeing them was palpable.

'He was standing at the checkout, and just keeled over,' she declared. 'I've put him in the recovery position, but I'm not qualified to do anything else. The first-aid course I went on—it only lasted four weekends—and—'

'You've done exactly the right thing,' Eli interrupted, smiling widely at her. 'We'll take over now.'

Brontë shook her head as the young first-aider turned bright red and walked away in a clear daze.

'Not fair. That poor girl was in a big enough spin before, but now you've got her practically hyperventilating.'

'Can I help it if I'm charming?' Eli protested, his blue eyes dancing, and Brontë only just restrained herself from sticking out her tongue at him.

Except he was probably right, she thought as she watched him begin the standard Glasgow coma scale assessment tests to check the man's overall physical condition. Being charming was undoubtedly as natural to Eli as breathing. So, unfortunately, was the fact he was as unreliable as the weather forecast.

But you like him.

Oh, I could, she thought, as she stared at his long, slender fingers, and, unbidden, and unwanted, an image came into her mind of those fingers touching her, caressing her. I could so easily like him very much indeed, but never in a million years would I allow herself to get involved with him. At least with the other men she'd dated she'd been completely unaware of what lay ahead, but with Eli Munroe she knew only too well.

'I'm not sure about this one,' Eli observed, sitting back on his heels. 'What do you think, Ms O'Brian?'

His expression was solemn but his eyes, Brontë noticed, were gleaming, and she knew why. He might only have performed two of the GCS tests on their patient so far but the man having achieved the lowest possible result both on the ability to open and close his eyes on command, and on responding verbally to questions, indicated he must be nearly at death's door but he had to be the healthiest-looking sick person she had ever seen.

'I'd recommend the reflexes test next, Mr Munroe,' she replied, and a suspicion of a smile appeared on Eli's lips.

Gently, he lifted the man's hand, positioned in directly over the man's nose, then let it drop. Magically, it didn't hit the man on his nose as it should have done if he really was unconscious, but landed neatly at his side, and Eli let out a deep, heartfelt sigh.

'I'm afraid it looks a lot more serious than I thought,' he declared, and Brontë had to bite down hard on her lip to quell the chuckle she could feel bubbling inside her.

She'd come across cases like this before in A and E. Sometimes the patients were mentally ill, or drunk, but most often they faked unconsciousness to get themselves out of a sticky situation and, judging by the amount of alcohol the man had in his shopping trolley, she strongly suspected he was trying to get away without paying for it.

'Eye socket test?' she suggested, and Eli winked across at her.

If the man truly was deeply unconscious he would scarcely react, but if he wasn't... Pushing hard against the upper part of his eye socket with your finger wouldn't damage his sight but, by heavens, he would certainly feel it.

He did. At the first push, the man's eyes flew open, and he sat up angrily, only to put his hand to his head with an unconvincing groan when he saw Brontë and Eli.

'I don't know what happened,' he murmured in a faltering voice. 'One minute I was about to pay for my groceries, and the next... I just came over all queer.'

'It can happen,' Eli agreed as he solicitously helped the man to his feet, 'which is why I think you should go straight home to bed. Forget all about your shopping, you can do it tomorrow.'

'But—'

'No, please, don't thank us,' Eli continued, steering the man towards the supermarket door. 'It's all in a day's—or should I say night's—work for us.'

That the man wanted to do anything *but* thank them was clear, but that he also didn't want to take on six feet two of muscular male was also apparent and, with a face like thunder, he walked out of the supermarket door and disappeared into the night.

'You know, it never ceases to amaze me how far some people will go to fake illness,' Brontë declared as she followed Eli back to their ambulance. 'I mean, if it was me, the last thing I'd want is someone performing a whole battery of tests on me if I knew I was perfectly okay.'

'Yeah, well, when you've been in this game as long as I have, nothing seems strange any more,' Eli replied. 'I'm just surprised *you're* surprised after seven years of A and E.'

She glanced across at him sharply. 'If this is your not very subtle way of wanting to know why I left, forget it.'

'Can't blame a bloke for trying,' he said with a broad smile, and she shook her head at him.

'You know, I don't think you actually *do* dump all your ex-girlfriends,' she observed. 'I think they dump you because you keep on asking the same old questions, and eventually they can't stand it any more.'

'Oh, very witty, very droll,' he said drily. 'And will you stop saying I dump women. I do *not* dump women. We just mutually decide when it's over.'

'Yeah, right,' she said, not even bothering to try to look as though she believed him. 'Do you want to know my theory as to why you're taking a three-month dating sabbatical?'

'Do I have a choice?'

'I think you got careless,' Brontë declared, ignoring the irritation in his voice. 'I think your last girlfriend got too close, and started bringing home wedding magazines, and stopping outside jewellers' windows to point out engagement rings, and that freaked you good and proper, and now you're trying to figure out where you went wrong.'

Eli's lips twitched into not quite a smile.

'That's not a bad guess.'

'And have you figured out where you went wrong?' she asked, and his smile became rueful.

'Not exactly. How long have you given up dating for?'

'Permanently.'

'*Permanently?*' he exclaimed. 'Hell, but someone sure did a number on you, didn't they?'

She was saved from answering by the bleep of their radio, but when she lifted the receiver, the caller sounded uncharacteristically nervous.

'I have a message for Eli,' the anonymous voice announced. 'Could you tell him Peg would like to see him asap.'

Brontë sighed with resignation as she switched off the receiver.

'Don't tell me,' she said, turning to Eli. 'Peg is yet another of your ex-girlfriends.'

He cleared his throat.

'Actually, she's a heroin addict. Turns tricks for a living. Male—female—doesn't matter to her so long as the punter will pay enough to fund her habit.'

Brontë blinked.

'And how do you know her?' she asked without thinking, then flushed scarlet when she realised how that might sound. 'Sorry—forget it—none of my business.'

'No, it's not,' he agreed. 'But Peg…' He chewed his lip, then seemed to come to a decision. 'She caught pneumonia two winters back. My partner, Frank, and I saw her lying in the street so we picked her up and took her to hospital. Ever since then…' Eli shrugged. 'She seems to feel she owes me something, so if a youngster tries to tag along with her, and her friends, she let's me know, and sometimes I'm able to help, to turn them around before it's too late.'

And I feel like the lowest form of pond life, Brontë thought as she stared at him awkwardly. She wished she hadn't jumped to conclusions. She wished even more she could figure out the man sitting next to her. One minute he was a completely shameless flirt, a serial dumper of women, then he unexpectedly turned into the Good Samaritan. It didn't make any sense. *He* didn't make any sense.

'Do you want to go and see her now?' she asked hesitantly.

'It's not a logged case, Brontë,' he replied. 'We're only supposed to answer logged calls, not personal ones.'

'And I didn't hear that,' she said. 'Where does Peg live?'

'Are you serious?' he said, and Brontë huffed impatiently.

'Just give me the address, Eli.'

'She…' He rubbed his chin awkwardly. 'She doesn't exactly "live" anywhere. She—and her friends—camp out most nights by Greyfriars Church.'

Greyfriars Church. It was hardly the most hospitable of places in the daytime but, on a freezing-cold November night, Brontë couldn't think of a more miserable place to be, and her opinion didn't change when they reached the church and she saw the black, locked gates.

'Where's your friend?' she asked as she and Eli got out of the ambulance.

'Inside.'

'Inside?' she repeated as he retrieved a medi-bag. 'You mean, she sleeps amongst the tombstones?'

'Yup.' Eli nodded, then his teeth gleamed white in the darkness. 'Not afraid of ghosts, I hope?'

Only my own, Brontë thought, but she didn't say it.

'I've always liked that statue of Greyfriars Bobby,' she said instead, pointing at the life-size figure of the little dog on a plinth in front of the church. 'My parents used to bring my brother, sister and I to see it when we were small, and tell us how Bobby came back every night for fourteen years to sleep on his owner's grave until he eventually died.'

'Yeah, well, putting up a statue to anyone—be it a person or a dog—is a lot easier than trying to help real, living people.'

Eli's voice sounded uncharacteristically hard, and bitter, and she glanced across at him curiously, but he wasn't looking at her. His eyes were scanning the graveyard, and then he nodded.

'There she is,' he said.

Following the direction of his gaze, Brontë saw a slim form flitting amongst the tombstones.

'How do we get in?' she asked. 'Do we have to climb over the railings, or…?'

'I know another way in.'

He did, and Brontë very soon wished he hadn't. It wasn't just the way the church seemed so much bigger and more ominous in the dark, nor the way the tombstones leant towards her like grasping, clutching fingers. It wasn't even the mort-safe coverings which had been installed over some of the graves by her Edinburgh forebears to prevent grave-robbers. It was the smell.

Sharp, acrid, and overpowering, it didn't matter how much she tried to hold her breath she couldn't escape the smell of unwashed bodies, and stale alcohol. It's just a smell, she told herself. Smells can't harm you, they can't hurt you, but, unbidden and unwanted, she felt her heart beginning to beat faster, could feel the all too familiar wave of panic rising within her, and she wrapped her arms around herself tightly.

'Must be well below zero tonight,' Eli observed, clearly misunderstanding her gesture.

She nodded.

'How many...' She swallowed hard. 'How many people sleep here every night?'

'It depends,' Eli replied. 'Sometimes ten—sometimes twenty.'

'How do they survive?' she exclaimed. 'How can they keep alive on nights like this? I would have thought—' She came to a sudden halt. Something warm, wet, and slimy was seeping through her left boot, encircling her toes, and she let out a small yelp. 'Oh, *yuck*! What have I just stood in?'

'Do you really want me to tell you?' Eli asked, and she shook her head quickly.

She didn't, especially as she already had a very strong suspicion what it was.

'Take my advice—'

'Buy some boots from Harper & Stolins in Cockburn Street,' she finished for him. 'I know, you said.'

'Yes, but this time *listen*,' he declared. 'We don't refuse to wear the regulation boots because we're picky. We don't wear them because they're rubbish, so get yourself a decent pair.'

She would, she thought, as she flexed her wet toes and grimaced. She would go to the shop at the end of this shift, but not until she'd had a very long, and very hot, shower.

'Okay, wait here,' Eli ordered. 'Peg and her friends...they know me, but you're a stranger, so it's best if I explain who you are.'

He was gone before she could argue, could tell him she didn't want to wait in this place on her own. Figures were emerging from behind the tombstones now, some of them coughing, all of them staggering, and though they looked merely curious, puzzled, she didn't know how long that would last, nor did she want to find out.

Anxiously, she searched the moonlit cemetery for Eli, but he was nowhere to be seen. Perhaps the newcomer had taken off, which would mean they could leave, too. She fervently hoped so. It was so cold here, so very cold. Dark, too, despite the moon. Dark and creepy, and she almost jumped out of her skin when she felt a hand clasp her shoulder.

'I didn't mean to frighten you,' Eli murmured, as she swore under her breath.

'Yeah, well, next time *warn* me, okay?' she said, trying to calm her thudding heart. 'What's the situation?'

'According to Peg, the newcomer's just a boy. He left his home in Aberdeenshire about a year ago—won't say why, but Peg reckons something bad happened. He got robbed of what little savings he had on his first night in Edinburgh, and with no money he couldn't pay for anywhere to live, and with no home address he couldn't get any benefits, so he's been living rough ever since.'

'What does Peg want us to do?'

'When did "I" become "us"?' Eli asked, and she could hear the smile in his voice.

'When I broke every rule in the EMDC manual by allowing this visit,' she replied, 'so quit stalling.'

'Basically she wants us to get him out of here. She thinks he has a bad cold, which is not good news. Pneumonia, or a severe chest infection, would mean we could take him to the Pentland which would get him off the streets for a while, but a cold…' He sighed. 'Peg's gone to ask if he'll let me examine him.'

The boy must have agreed because, out of the gloom, Brontë could see a white hand beckoning to them, and quickly she followed Eli as he picked his way through the tombstones, keeping as close to him as she could, so she almost collided into his back when he came to a sudden halt by one of the bigger mausoleums.

'Is this him?' she whispered, only to instantly feel stupid because, of course, it had to be, and yet…

She had expected to see a young man but the person sitting hunched on the ground in front of them, dressed in threadbare trainers, thin denim trousers, and a tattered wine-coloured jacket, didn't even look old enough to have left school. How on earth had he survived if he'd been sleeping rough for a year?

'What's your name, son?' Eli murmured as he crouched down in front of the boy, seemingly heedless of the broken glass, and discarded syringes, glinting in the moonlight.

With an effort, the boy raised his head. His skin was stretched tightly across his cheekbones, and there were dark shadows under his eyes, but though those eyes looked tired and scared, Brontë didn't think he was taking drugs. At least, not yet.

'I'm…John,' the boy replied. 'John Smith.'

Yeah, right, Brontë thought, and I'm Mary, Queen of Scots.

'I understand you have a bad cold,' Eli continued, 'and you've agreed to let me examine you?'

A defeated shrug was the only reply, and Eli took a stethoscope out of the bag Brontë was holding out to him.

'How old are you, John?' Brontë asked, and the boy's eyes slid warily away.

'Eighteen,' he said. 'I'm eighteen.'

'Fourteen more like,' she could not help but reply, and the boy rounded on her angrily.

'Look, I didn't ask you to come,' he said. 'You came of your own accord, so I don't need the third degree!'

Eli shook his head warningly at Brontë, then turned back to John.

'Fair enough,' he said softly, 'no third degree.'

Quickly, he sounded the young man's thin chest, and took his pulse while Brontë stood silently by. So, too, she noticed, did Peg. Not close enough to see what Eli was doing, but close enough to help if she was needed. Which meant she was on guard, Brontë realised. On guard because everyone there would know Eli was carrying drugs, and nervously she moved closer to him.

'How is his chest?' she asked when Eli had finished his examination.

'He has a cold, nothing serious,' he replied.

She could hear the disappointment in his voice. She felt it herself, and quickly she hunkered down beside him and the boy.

'John, listen to me,' she began. 'Why don't you go home? I'll buy you the train ticket—'

'*No!*' the young boy broke in vehemently. 'I'm not going home!'

'But how are you managing for food?' Brontë demanded. 'You've no money, no means of getting any.'

'People…when they get takeaways…they don't always eat it all,' the boy replied. 'They throw away some of it, so I get by. I just…'

'Just what?' Brontë prompted, and the boy raised his dark eyes to hers.

'I'm so scared all the time. Scared someone will come along and set fire to me when I'm sleeping. It happens,' he continued, hearing Brontë's sharp intake of breath. 'One of the older homeless guys… He told me it happened to one of his mates, so I don't sleep. I just keep on walking, and walking, and I get so tired, so very tired.'

'Okay, John, listen to me,' Eli declared. 'You have to sleep and the safest place is businesses with flat roofs. No one will be able to see you up there, and they usually have a raised part to stop you rolling off, so as long as you're not stoned or drunk you'll be safe.'

The boy nodded. 'Flat roofs. Anywhere else?'

'A bathroom with a keypad is the best of all,' Eli replied. 'A lot of big businesses, and shops, have them. Get yourself as clean as you can, and hang about until you've found out what the code is. Watch for a night to check cleaning crews don't work outside the normal business hours and it will be yours for ages if you leave it clean without a trace of you having been there.'

'Right.' The boy's eyes met Eli's. 'Thanks.'

Slowly, Eli straightened up and Brontë could see his breath on the cold night air, the sparkle of frost on the roofs. If it was so cold now, how much colder was it going to get as the night progressed?

'Eli…' He wasn't listening to her, he was already walking away, and she hurried after him, stumbling slightly on the uneven ground. 'Eli, wait!'

He did and, when he turned to face her, his face was harsh, angry.

'How old would you say Peg was?' he asked.

Brontë frowned. She hadn't paid much attention.

'Fifty-five…sixty?' She hazarded.

'She's thirty-two.'

Brontë glanced back over her shoulder to where Peg was still standing beside John. Even in the dark she could see most of the woman's teeth were gone, her hair was lank, and stringy, and she had the running nose, extreme restlessness, and dilated pupils of someone who desperately needed another 'fix.'

'John—or whatever his name really is—will be like that in a year if we don't get him out,' Eli continued. 'So many of the people here…' He waved his hand at the men and women clustered together. 'It's too late for them. No matter what help we throw at them, or what services are provided, it's too late, but there's still hope for John and if we can save one...'

'I have some money on me,' Brontë began, digging deep into her pocket. 'It's not much—about twenty pounds—'

'Which will get him into a homeless shelter, and feed him for three—maybe four—days, and then what?' Eli interrupted. 'He needs long-term help. He needs to be in hospital for a few days so social services can assess him, put a plan in place.' His eyes met hers. 'How willing are you to break yet another of the EMDC manual rules?'

'Right now, I'd happily break the lot of them,' she answered, 'but, Eli, if all he has is a cold we'll get our heads in our hands if we turn up at the Pentland with him.'

'Not if you know the right person to go to.'

'And you do?' she asked and, when his mouth curved into a wide grin, she shook her head. 'Stupid question. Of course you do. What's her name?'

'Dr Helen Carter. She works Tuesdays and Thursdays in A and E at the Pentland, and she'll help.'

Dr Carter did. Within minutes of their arrival, she had John whisked up to a ward, and had called the social services.

'I'm not guaranteeing anything, Eli,' she declared, 'but with some luck, and a little bit of help from the Almighty, perhaps we can set that young lad back on track.'

'Helen, I love you.' Eli beamed, and Dr Carter shook her head and laughed.

'Away with you. I'm old enough to be your mother.'

Which didn't, Brontë noticed, stop Helen Carter blushing when Eli kissed her cheek, but she said nothing as she followed him out of A and E because she was too busy thinking.

He'd warned her not to judge him by his outward appearance, and he'd been right. Who *was* this man, what made him tick, and what else was going on in his head he didn't allow the rest of the world to see? Yes, he was a serial womaniser, but he also cared very deeply, not only about the people they collected who were very ill, but also about those who were down on their luck. It was as though there were two completely separate Eli Munroes, and no matter how hard she tried she just couldn't reconcile the two of them.

'The callers at Oxgangs,' she said as they got into the ambulance, 'do they know who Peg is?'

He shook his head. 'They think the same as you did, that she's an ex-girlfriend. Only Frank—the guy I'm normally partnered with—knows.'

But *why*? she wanted to ask. Why didn't he tell people, why keep something like this—an act of great kindness—hidden?

'Eli—'

'I haven't thanked you yet, and I should have done,' he interrupted as she put the ambulance in gear.

'What for?' Brontë asked.

'Breaking the rules.'

'I couldn't do anything else,' Brontë replied as she eased the ambulance out onto the main road before picking up speed.

'Yes, you could,' he said softly. 'A lot of people…when they see down-and-outs begging on the streets, sleeping in cardboard boxes… They think, failures, losers, not my problem.'

'I guess I'm all too aware it doesn't take much to put any one of us in the same position,' Brontë murmured. 'You just need to lose your job, and with no pay cheque you can't pay your mortgage payments, or the rent on your flat, and once you've got nowhere to live…'

'It's welcome to dead-end alley.' Eli sighed. 'With all too often no way back, no way out.'

Brontë glanced across at him, and took a deep breath.

'What you were saying to John about safe places for him to sleep,' she began. 'It seemed—not that it's any of my business, or anything—but it almost sounded like you'd had, you know, personal experience of living rough.'

Eli's face tightened. 'You're right. It's none of your business.'

'Okay.' She nodded. 'Sorry.'

For a moment he said nothing, then his face relaxed slightly, and one corner of his mouth reluctantly turned up.

'You're a very dangerous woman, Brontë O'Brian.'

'Me—dangerous?' she echoed, confused. 'How?'

'Anyone else would have probed, and cajoled, and tried to get an answer out of me, and I would have bitten their head off, but you simply shrug, and say, "Okay," which almost makes me want to explain.'

'And that would be a bad thing?' she said, and heard him sigh.

'A very bad thing.'

She wanted to ask him why, but what right did she have to ask him anything? They weren't friends, she scarcely knew him, and—and it was a very big *and*—she doubted whether he would give her an answer anyway. So she drove silently past the National Library of Scotland, over the South Bridge, turned right into the Cowgate where a gang of youths seemed to be fooling about, and then suddenly her whole world went black, and she hit the brakes in complete panic.

'Don't break, *don't* break!' Eli yelled. 'Just keep your steering wheel straight.'

She did as he ordered even though all of her instincts were telling her to push the brake pedal straight to the floor, and suddenly she could see again. Without her realising it, Eli had switched on the windscreen wipers and, though the windscreen was smeared and dark, at least she could see through it, and she pulled the ambulance to a halt and leant her head on the steering wheel.

'What the *hell* happened?' She gasped as her thudding heart slowed to a gallop.

'Beer bottle. Those kids we were passing, one of them must have thrown it at the windscreen.'

'But that's...*insane!*' she exclaimed. 'Didn't they realise...didn't they think... I could have swerved straight into them!'

'Doubt if it even crossed their minds,' Eli replied, pulling a duster out of the glove compartment.

How could he be so indifferent? How could he simply sit there as though it was an every-night occasion? Unless...

She swallowed shakily. 'Does...does this happen a lot?'

'Depends upon what you mean by a lot,' he replied. 'If there's nothing interesting on TV, gangs of young lads tend to congregate around the streets, and then they get bored.' He frowned. 'It's pretty unusual, though, to get a full bottle of beer thrown at us. Normally they're empty.'

'And is that supposed to make me feel *better*?' she said, her voice rising in pitch.

'At least they didn't deliberately run out in front of you,' he observed. 'Scared the hell out of me the first time it happened. Apparently, you earn extra kudos from your mates if you can run across the road in front of an ambulance when it's on a code red, with its siren flashing.'

'Fascinating,' she said, desperately trying to smile, and failing miserably, and then her heart leapt back into her mouth when Eli suddenly swore. 'What is it—what's wrong?'

'They're still there—the gang,' he said grimly. 'And they are about to get a very large piece of my mind.'

He was going to get out of the ambulance and confront them, and she could see the young men in her mirror, laughing, jeering, bottles clutched in their hands, and, before she could stop herself, she grabbed hold of Eli's arm.

'*Don't!*'

'Brontë, I'm just going to talk to them,' he said, trying to shrug off her hand which only made her hold on even tighter.

'You are *not* going out there!' she all but screamed at him. 'You're staying where you are, you hear me?'

'Brontë, calm down,' he said, worry replacing the irritation in his eyes. 'Look, I won't go out if you don't want to me to.'

'You promise?' she said convulsively, and gently he prised her fingers from his arm.

'They've gone now, anyway,' he said, 'and I want you to take some deep breaths. Lots and lots of deep breaths.'

She could hear it in his voice. The same tone she'd always used when she was dealing with panicking kids in A and E, and it mortified her beyond belief. Somehow she had to get a grip of herself, or she was going to have a full-blown panic attack right in front of him.

'I'm fine now—I'm okay now,' she said as calmly as she could, and he shook his head.

'Coffee,' he said. 'You need coffee, and I'll drive.'

She wanted to protest, to tell him she was perfectly capable of driving, but she knew one glance at her shaking hands would tell him she was lying, but getting out of the ambulance… She didn't know if her legs would take her that far, and he clearly read her mind.

'When I get out, you slide over the gear-stick into the passenger seat.'

'But—'

He'd already gone, and awkwardly she did as he'd ordered, forcing her legs to work, and forcing herself not to shout at Eli to get back into the safety of the ambulance when he paused to clean the windscreen. Neither did she ask where they were going, because she knew where it would be and, when he pulled the ambulance up outside Tony's, she was sufficiently in control of herself to manage a crooked smile.

'Sorry about that,' she said, wishing her voice didn't still sound so shaky. 'I just…the bottle… I hadn't expected it, you see.'

'Do you want your usual?'

She nodded, but when he'd gone into Tony's she shut her eyes tight. Her usual. After just two days he'd called her coffee her 'usual,' as though she was beginning to belong to this station, but she didn't, and it wasn't just because she'd be leaving in a few days. She didn't belong anywhere near medical services, not any more.

'I got you a doughnut as well as a coffee,' Eli said when he returned. 'I figured you probably needed some carbs and sugar.'

'Thanks,' she said, then noticed the chocolate biscuit in his hand. 'No hamburger for you tonight?'

'I didn't want to run the risk of you throwing up,' he replied, and she gripped her polystyrene cup of coffee tightly.

'I'm okay now,' she insisted. 'Stop fussing, will you?'

He did. In fact, he said nothing at all for a good five minutes, but she was all too aware he was watching her from the corner of his eye and, when she'd finished the doughnut, and half emptied her cup of coffee, he turned towards her.

'Okay, are you going to tell me what that was all about?'

Pretending not to understand him wasn't an option, but neither did she want to tell him the truth.

'I admit I lost it a bit when that bottle hit the window,' she conceded, 'but, come on, Eli, any normal person would have reacted the same way. If your world suddenly goes black, and you can't see anything, and you're driving…'

'Good attempt, Brontë, but no sale,' he said. 'I thought you looked peaky in Greyfriars but I put that down to the cold. I know you got a terrible fright when the bottle hit the windscreen, but what I want to know is why you freaked out when I wanted to get out of the ambulance and confront those yobs.'

'There were a lot of them,' she protested. 'I was afraid you might get hurt.'

He sighed, and pushed his black hair back from his forehead.

'Brontë, I am not being nosy, I'm not being intrusive, but you've got to look at this from my point of view. You're riding with me, so don't you think I have a right to know if some situations are going to make you panic?'

He was right, he did have a right to know, but she didn't want to talk about it, talking about it only brought it all back.

'Eli…'

'It's got something to do with why you left A and E, hasn't it?'

She stared at the windscreen. She could still see some stray streaks of beer he'd missed, and there were little bits of lint on the windscreen from the duster he'd used, and she didn't want to say anything but she knew she had to.

'I was on duty one Saturday night,' she began, her voice jerky, low. 'We had the usual crowd in. People who had drunk too much, drug addicts who had collapsed in the street, ordinary members of the public who had hurt themselves and who looked as though they'd rather be anywhere but there, but they needed help.'

'A typical Saturday night, in other words.' He nodded.

'Pretty much,' she murmured. 'And then…' She took a steadying breath, trying only to remember the facts, and not how she had felt, but it didn't work, it never did. 'This gang came in. They were all drunk, and one of them… He'd gashed his hand pretty badly, and I was dressing it, and he was screaming I was a bitch, deliberately hurting him.'

'And?' Eli prompted gently when she came to a halt.

'His friends… They began crowding into the cubicle. They were pushing me, jostling me, pulling at my clothes, and then one of them…' She gripped her coffee tightly. 'One of them pulled a knife on me.'

'Nasty,' Elijah murmured, his eyes never leaving her face. 'He hurt you.'

It was a statement, not a question, and she tried to smile and failed.

'He punctured my lung. I was off work for four months, and when I went back… The first gang of drunks we had in… I froze, couldn't go anywhere near them, so that was it. Nursing career down the toilet, but with rent to pay and bills coming in I needed a job, so when I saw this one advertised I thought I'd apply, and I got it.'

'Did you have counselling after the attack?'

A bitter laugh came from her. '"Face your fear, and then you'll conquer it." That's what the shrink said, and I know he's right, but what do you do when you can't actually face the fear, when every part of you is shrieking, Run, just run.'

Eli cleared his throat.

'Brontë, you do realise that, when you're out with me, the odds are virtually one hundred per cent that we'll encounter drunks.'

'But I won't be treating them,' she pointed out. 'I won't have to touch them. I'm not denying that being near someone drunk makes me uneasy, but as long as it's not a crowd, a gang, and I don't have to touch them, I can cope.' She met his gaze. 'What are you going to do?'

Her grey eyes were unhappy, but he could see resignation in them, too, and, for a second he didn't understand her, and then it hit him. He could get her fired. That was what she was thinking, and, by heavens, *he could*. All he had to do was take her back to the station, explain how she'd freaked out, and she'd be out of his hair for good.

Except he wouldn't do it. If he told George what had happened, she'd have no job, no money coming in, and she looked so damn small sitting next to him, small and beaten, and he hated seeing her look beaten. She'd been born to be sassy, snippy, and if he shafted her now, after all she'd been through, what kind of man would that make him?

'Well, when you've finished your coffee, you and I are going to go kerb crawling until we get a call,' he said.

'But I thought…'

'Take a tip from one who knows,' he said lightly, 'don't think. Thinking is a very bad idea. Now, finish your coffee.'

She pulled a handkerchief out of her pocket, blew her nose vigorously, and then she smiled at him.

A big, wide smile that completely altered her face, making it soft, and luminous, almost pretty, and he found himself smiling back. Found himself noticing, too, that, under the lamplight, her hair wasn't a dull brown after all, but had little strands of gold in it, and her eyes weren't simply grey but actually a pale silver but, as he continued to stare at her, he suddenly realised something else. He wanted to reach out, gather her into his arms and tell her he'd make everything all right, and that was *insane*.

What on earth was happening to him? he wondered, clasping his hands together tightly to prevent them from carrying out the thought. He didn't 'do' protective, any more than he 'did' apologies, and just because she was sitting there looking so tiny, her lips parted in a wide smile…

Feeling protective of a woman was right up there alongside involvement, commitment, on the list of things he'd spent a lifetime avoiding.

'Eli?'

Uncertainty was slowly replacing the gratitude in her eyes, and he shook his head to clear it.

'Well, I owe you one for Peg, don't I?' he said, and saw her smile disappear, and hurt replace it.

'I wouldn't have told anyone about her,' she said, her voice low, subdued.

He knew she wouldn't, and he felt like a heel for saying

what he had, but somehow he had to distance himself from this woman because he could feel an abyss opening up in front of him. A yawning abyss which would be oh-so easy to fall into and, when a caller's voice echoed over the airwaves, he grabbed the receiver like a lifeline.

CHAPTER THREE

Thursday, 12:06 a.m.

SOMETHING was badly wrong, Brontë decided as she drove down St John's Street, then turned left. At first, when she'd come on duty this evening, she'd thought it was just her, that she was bound to feel a little awkward, a little uncomfortable, after her panic attack yesterday, but it was more than that, much more.

'Take a sharp right at the junction. It's the quickest way to Chambers Street, but watch the corner. The roads themselves are okay, but the pavements and street corners are pretty icy tonight.'

She smiled her thanks across at Eli, but he wasn't looking at her and that, she realised, was the problem in a nutshell. Whenever she'd glanced in his direction this evening he hadn't met her gaze, and yet whenever she looked away she knew his eyes were upon her.

He thinks you're a fruit cake, her mind whispered. *He's had second thoughts about what happened yesterday, and he's decided you're a fruit cake.*

Which was so unfair. It wasn't as though she'd lost it at any point tonight. They'd been sent out to attend a woman who had been having a bad asthma attack, a child who had scalded himself, and an elderly gentleman with a severe chest infection, and she'd behaved completely professionally the whole time, but he had clearly decided she was trouble, and his tiptoeing around her was getting to her big time.

'I don't see anyone lying in the street,' she said, scanning the road ahead of them, 'but Dispatch definitely said Chambers Street. Could they have been given the wrong address?'

'Maybe.'

Well, that was short and sweet, she thought irritably. Last night, he'd been so kind, so solicitous, and she'd managed the rest of the shift without incident, but tonight it was like sitting beside a stranger. A polite, distant stranger who only ever spoke in monosyllables.

'Could that be him?' she declared, seeing a sudden movement beside one of the buildings. 'He's not lying in the road, but he's walking oddly, like he's injured.'

'Or drunk,' Eli murmured. 'Dispatch said the caller couldn't stay at the scene which usually means a drunk. If someone has suffered a heart attack, or an epileptic fit, passers-by tend to stay with them, but a drunk… No one wants to get involved.'

'Drunk, or not, I think he's hurt his leg,' Brontë replied as she drew the ambulance to a halt at the kerbside. 'See how he's dragging it?'

Eli said nothing. He simply retrieved a medi-bag, but, when he opened the cab door, he hesitated momentarily.

'There's no need for you to come with me,' he observed. 'I can deal with this.'

He might well be able to, she decided, but if she couldn't cope with one drunk she was in considerably worse shape than she thought.

'I'm coming,' she said firmly, and he muttered something under his breath which she very much doubted was, 'Terrific,' and she exhaled sharply.

Why didn't he just come right out and tell her that riding with him wasn't going to work? It was so clearly what he was thinking, and she'd far rather he simply said it instead of skirting round her like she was some sort of ticking time bomb.

'Eli—'

'He's gone over,' Eli interrupted as a thud echoed round the empty street.

The man had. He was now flat on his back on the pavement, and he'd taken a dustbin with him, sending its contents spilling out onto the icy pavement.

'The street cleaners are going to love this when they come on duty tomorrow.' She smiled, but no returning smile greeted her words.

In fact, she might just as well have been talking to the dustbin, she thought with annoyance, as Eli walked away and she gingerly quickened her pace over the frosty pavement to catch up with him.

'Drunk for sure,' Eli observed when they reached the man, 'but you were right about the leg. My guess is he's fallen on some broken glass.'

It would have been Brontë's guess, too, as Eli pulled some scissors, swabs and antiseptic out of his bag. She could see a jagged tear in the man's trouser leg through which blood was slowly seeping, and she could also see some tiny shards of glass.

'Looks like a stitch job to me,' she said.

Eli nodded. 'And I doubt he's kept his tetanus shots up to date so we'd better take him to A and E after I've cleaned that gash.'

He was going to need more than just the gash cleaned, Brontë thought ruefully when the man suddenly rolled over and was violently sick down the front of his jacket. A complete bath would be more in order, but that obviously wasn't uppermost in Eli's mind.

'Look, you really don't have to stay with me,' he said. 'Why don't you go back to the cab?'

She counted to ten, but it didn't help. Okay, so the alcohol fumes emanating from the man would have been enough to knock most people over at ten paces, but she was coping, and she deeply resented the implication that he thought she wasn't.

'I'll stay,' she said.

'There's no need,' Eli insisted, as he began bagging up the soiled swabs he had used. 'I can get him into the ambulance by myself.'

'Oh, really?' she retorted, unable to curb her sarcasm. 'So you're going to lift a twenty-stone man all by yourself on a pavement that's like glass? I don't think so.'

Quickly, she bent down and put her hands under the man's shoulders, exhaling through her nose to keep her breathing to a minimum. One drunk, she told herself, as she felt the familiar quickening of her heart. It's one drunk. One virtually comatose drunk, and you can handle that. You have to for your own self-respect.

'Brontë, you don't have to do this,' Eli said gently, his eyes concerned, and she swore under her breath.

'I'd do it a lot faster if you helped,' she snapped. 'Or are you just going to stand there and watch?'

She saw his jaw clench, but she sure as heck wasn't going to apologise. There was a fine line between watching out for her, and constantly treating her like a stick of dynamite, and he had well and truly crossed that line.

'Drive fast,' Eli said once they got the man safely into the back of the ambulance, and he climbed in beside him. 'If he throws up again, we'll be stuck with a two-hour lay-off at the station until the cleaners can disinfect the ambulance.'

She nodded, and, within ten minutes, the man had been delivered into the arms of an A and E staff nurse at the Pentland who looked anything but pleased by the new arrival.

'Apparently that's the fourth drunk one of our ambulances

has brought in tonight,' Eli explained. 'Which means ED7's name is now well and truly mud amongst the nursing staff.'

'Some nights in A and E are like that,' Brontë replied as she drove out of the ambulance bay in front of the hospital. 'We used to get cycles at the Waverley. One night it would be a rash of heart attacks, the next a whole host of broken legs. One summer—' she chuckled as she remembered '—it was wall-to-wall food poisoning. We ended up using everything from kidney dishes to buckets for people to be sick in.'

Eli didn't laugh. He didn't do anything but stare fixedly out of the window, and she gritted her teeth.

'I can't believe it will soon be Christmas,' she said, deliberately changing the subject. 'Just twenty-eight shopping days left, according to the newspapers.'

'Yes.'

'Do you spend Christmas with your family, or on your own?' she continued determinedly.

'On my own.'

Look, work with me here, she thought, crunching the gears as she turned the corner at the bottom of the road. I'm trying to make conversation, but I'm getting nothing back in return. She risked a quick glance at him but all she could see was his stiff, rigid back. Dammit, even his body language suggested, Stay back—keep away.

'It's almost twenty to three,' she said. 'What say we take an early break, head for Tony's?'

Eli cleared his throat.

'Actually, I was wondering whether we shouldn't perhaps go back to the station tonight for our coffee. I mean, you haven't met any of the other paramedics, or talked to them,' he continued, not meeting her gaze, 'so I was wondering whether we should give Tony's a miss this evening.'

Which she might have bought if he hadn't already told her that all of the ambulance crews took their coffee breaks at Tony's. He just didn't want to be alone in the cab with her, she thought grimly. Well, enough was enough, and she was going to tell him so.

Swiftly, she turned into College Street, brought the ambulance to a halt, and switched off the engine.

'What's wrong?' Eli asked.

'You—me,' she said. 'We need to talk.'

His lips quirked unexpectedly.

'Isn't that normally my line?'

'Yeah, well, you know what they say about the old ones being the best ones,' she declared. 'We need to talk about what happened yesterday.'

His smile disappeared in an instant and she saw wariness creep into his eyes.

'What's there to talk about?' he said.

'Eli, me driving you… It is not going to work if you keep watching me as though you're terrified I'm suddenly going to strip off all my clothes, put my knickers on my head and run manically through The Meadows. And if you dare to say, "That I would like to see,"' she warned as one corner of his lips curved, 'I *swear* I will hit you.'

'Okay, I won't say it,' he replied. 'I might think it….'

'*Eli!*'

'Okay, okay. Is that what you think I've been doing?' he continued. 'Worrying, about you?'

'Oh, come on,' she protested. 'This is the first time you've actually looked me in the eye all night, and you're skirting round me like I'm an unexploded keg of gunpowder which is going to blow at any moment. What else am I supposed to think?'

She was right, he thought as he stared back at her. Those strange feelings he'd experienced yesterday… He'd simply been worried. Understandably worried. After all, it wouldn't only be her neck on the line if she had a complete panic attack while they were out on the road, it would be his, too, because he was covering up for her.

And what about you noticing what a lovely smile she has, and her eyes aren't really grey but quicksilver? a nagging voice asked at the back of his mind.

Sexual deprivation, he told himself firmly. He'd been celibate for the past two months and, for a guy who had always enjoyed a regular sex life, that was bound to take its toll. In fact, it was a miracle it hadn't happened before, and, once Brontë had completed her report, and left the station, and he started dating again, everything would fall into its proper perspective.

'Eli?'

She looked both irritated, and annoyed, and relief flooded through him. He wasn't losing it. He wasn't falling into any abyss. His feelings had been *normal*, and he smiled.

'You're right. Memo to self—quit worrying, kid gloves off, and we go back to the way we were. You chewing my head off, and me refusing to take it.'

'Since when did I chew your head off?' she demanded, and he grinned.

'Virtually from your first hello.'

'Well, you deserved it,' she said. 'All that flattery… Maybe it works on other women, but it sure as heck doesn't work on me.'

'No, it doesn't, does it?' he said, his blue eyes suddenly thoughtful. 'I wonder why that is?'

Because I know what you are, she was tempted to retort, but she didn't, not least because it wasn't true. The more she got to know him, the less she was able to puzzle him out. Like his kindness to Peg, a kindness he wanted no one to discover. His kindness to her last night when he must have thought she was half demented. Even the way he could be bothered to worry about her tonight—though the worrying had become deeply irritating—was completely unexpected.

'I told you before you weren't my type,' she said lightly, 'which probably explains why your charm offensives don't work on me. Plus,' she added, feeling impelled to embroider the lie, 'I've always preferred blonds to brunettes.'

His eyebrows rose with interest.

'So the guy who did a number on you, the one who made you decide to give up dating permanently, was blond, was he?'

Damn, that would teach her to embellish.

'Stop fishing,' she declared, considerably flustered. 'I told you before it was none of your business, and it isn't.'

'I told you why I gave up dating for three months,' he pointed out, 'so I reckon it's only fair you tell me your reason.'

'You didn't tell me,' she countered. 'I figured it out myself, so that doesn't count, and, anyway, did nobody ever tell you life—'

'Isn't fair?' He smiled. 'Yup, you did, and that's no answer, so tell me.'

Right now, she realised with dismay, she would probably have told him anything because he was smiling at her. Not the normal smile she'd seen so many times since she'd started working with him, but the smile the women he'd dated always remembered so wistfully, and she could see exactly what they meant. That smile was a doozy. It was a smile which said, Tell me everything. A smile that said, I really want to know all about you, and she took an uneven, shaky breath. Oh, criminy, but even when he was faking interest—and she knew he was faking it—the combination of his deep blue eyes and that smile was dynamite.

'Silence isn't an option, Brontë,' he continued as she stared at him, horribly aware she probably looked slack-jawed. 'I want an answer.'

Damn, but she couldn't even remember what the question was.

'Eli…'

'A38, could you give us your current position, please?'

'Typical,' Eli complained as Brontë grabbed the receiver

with relief. 'Just when I thought I might finally be getting an answer. But that doesn't mean you're off the hook, O'Brian,' he added with a grin. 'I don't give up easily.'

He obviously didn't, Brontë thought, but right now it wasn't his persistence which concerned her. She was too busy desperately trying to get her brain back into gear.

'A38, here,' she said into the receiver, and was pleased to hear her voice sounded, if not normal, at least relatively calm. 'We're in College Street.'

'Then we have a cat A for you,' the caller replied. 'Number 49, Holyrood Gate. Roland Finlay. Fifty-five years old, fallen out of bed, possible "suspended."'

'What's a "suspended"?' Brontë asked as she started the ignition.

'Someone who is either dead, or has had a heart attack,' Eli explained. 'Hit the siren, and go.'

Brontë did. She reversed swiftly out of College Street, then headed east, their blue siren flashing and wailing as she went.

'Up the siren's strength to max,' Eli advised, 'and if you meet any traffic drive straight down the middle of the road. Now is the not the time for any "After you, Claude" driving, now is the time for speed, and if other vehicles don't get out of your way they take the consequences.'

Which sounded scary. In fact, when she'd been taking her LGV C1 driving lessons, she'd been worried she might freeze completely if she ever had to drive at breakneck speed through the Edinburgh streets but, to her amazement, she discovered it was actually downright exhilarating.

'You're enjoying this, aren't you?' Eli chuckled as she let out a small whoop of triumph after she'd squeezed between two cars with scarcely a millimetre to spare, then shot straight through some red traffic lights without even breaking.

'Yup.' She beamed.

'Maybe you should retrain to be a paramedic.'

'Yeah, right,' she said drily. 'Except somehow I doubt there'd be much call for a paramedic who can only treat kids and little old ladies.'

'You'll get over your fear,' he said softly. 'Trust me, it will happen.'

Trust him? If anyone had suggested to her two days ago that she should trust Elijah Munroe she would have laughed in their face. Everything she had been told, everything she'd seen of the way he treated women, made the idea of 'trust' a ludicrous one, and yet… Maybe he was right. Not about re-training to become a paramedic—she wasn't at all convinced the work would suit her—but, if she could conquer her fear, maybe she could go back to doing the work she had always loved, and the thought made her smile.

'What's funny?' he asked.

'Nothing—not important,' she replied, then added, 'We're in Holyrood Gate. Any idea where number 49 might be?'

'I can see number 19,' Eli said, peering out of the window, 'but that's 24, and that's 26. Jeez, was it an architect on drugs who allotted these numbers?'

Brontë drove to the very top of the street, with Eli scanning every block they passed but, when she turned at the top of the road to retrace their steps, he pounded his fist angrily on the dashboard.

'Why don't people put bigger number signs on their homes?' he exclaimed. 'Forget the trendy, dump the discreet, because when it's an emergency like this people like us need to know where the heck you are!'

Brontë said nothing, feeling perhaps now was not the right time to tell him her own flat number was every bit as small as the ones they had passed.

'Number 16, number 11,' she murmured as she drove slowly back down the street, 'number 9… Could it be inside that block there—the one with 45 on the wall?'

'It could be.' Eli nodded. 'But what's the bet 49 is on the

third floor, and there's no elevator? Every paramedic's worst nightmare when it's a "suspended."'

'Right now, my nightmare is finding somewhere to park,' Brontë said, with frustration. 'It's bumper-to-bumper cars out there.'

'Then park in the middle of the road.'

'But we'll block the street.'

'And someone might be dying, so *park*.'

She did and, after they'd pulled their med-bags, and a carry-chair, out of the ambulance, they hit the ground running. Or at least they would have done if Mr Finlay's home had been on the ground floor but, as Eli had predicted, number 49 was the third-floor flat, and there was no elevator.

'I'm going to have to start taking some exercise,' Brontë declared breathlessly as she followed Eli round the landing on the second floor and saw to her annoyance that he didn't look even slightly winded.

'Running naked through The Meadows would give you some,' he replied, throwing her a grin over his shoulder.

'You're not going to let me forget that, are you?' she said, easing the defibrillator she was carrying onto her other shoulder.

'Nope. And I still haven't discovered why you've given up dating, but I will.'

She shook her head, but inwardly she was smiling. It was so good to have him talking to her again, so good not to feel awkward and uncomfortable in his presence. Okay, so his special smiles might make her feel considerably flustered, but she would rather deal with them than the wary silence she'd had to endure all night.

'I heard the siren,' a middle-aged woman declared when she opened the door of number 49 before they'd even knocked. 'It's my husband. He's not breathing. Please help him. Please, *please*, help him.'

Swiftly, Brontë followed Eli and Mrs Finlay through to the

bedroom and saw Mr Finlay lying in a crumpled heap beside the bed.

'I don't know what happened,' Mrs Finlay continued, panic plain in her face. 'I was watching the late-night movie on TV, and heard this loud thud. I think he was perhaps going to the toilet, but I don't know, I honestly don't know.'

Eli was already connecting Mr Finlay to the heart monitor and within seconds it was obvious the man was in PEA— pulseless electrical activity. Mr Finlay's heart wasn't moving any blood around his body, and unless they could get his heart moving again he would be dead within minutes.

'Do you want me to do the chest compressions, or to set up the Ambu bag?' Brontë asked.

'Ambu bag,' Eli replied.

The chest compressions he was applying would push some oxygen to Mr Finlay's essential organs, but he needed those lungs full of oxygen, and fast. He also needed life-saving drugs, and she could see Eli searching for a suitable vein in Mr Finlay's arm after she'd affixed the Ambu bag and, instinctively, she glanced at her watch. Their window of opportunity for bringing Mr Finlay back was narrowing by the minute.

'ET?' she suggested, and Eli nodded.

A vein would have been much faster, but inserting an endotracheal tube into Mr Finlay's throat, and giving him the drugs that way, was better than nothing but just as Eli had successfully inserted the tube, the heart monitor suddenly let out a shrill warning.

'What does that mean?' Mrs Finlay asked frantically. 'That noise…those lines and numbers on the screen… What do they mean?'

That her husband had gone into VF—ventricular fibrillation—when the heart went into total chaotic activity, and things had just got a hundred times worse, Brontë thought, but she didn't say it, and neither did Eli.

'It's just a small blip, Mrs Finlay, nothing for you to be concerned about,' he said instead with a reassuring smile as he instantly resumed CPR. 'We just need to give your husband's heart rhythm a little boost, that's all.'

'But—'

'Could you do something for us, Mrs Finlay?' Eli continued quickly. 'Obviously, we're going to need to take your husband to hospital, so could you collect some blankets for us to keep him warm? Oh, and some flasks full of boiling water would be very helpful, too,' he added as Mrs Finlay turned to go.

Brontë knew they had plenty of blankets in the ambulance, and they most certainly didn't need any flasks of boiling water, but she also knew what Eli was doing. He was trying to get Mrs Finlay away from the scene rather than allowing her to watch them attempting to resuscitate her husband. It was something she'd never had to do in A and E. In A and E, a patient's family was always kept firmly outside, away from any medical procedures which could be upsetting, but here, on the front line, the ambulance services didn't have that luxury.

'How high do you want the power?' she said, once Mrs Finlay had gone.

'Two hundred joules,' Eli replied.

There was no tension in his voice, no indication at all of the seriousness of the situation, and Brontë could not help but admire his skill and professionalism as she swiftly rubbed the defibrillator paddles with electrical conducting gel, ensuring the gel completely covered the surface of the paddles, so Mr Finlay's skin wouldn't be badly burned. Calm, and unflappable, as well as unexpectedly kind and thoughtful, he was exactly the kind of nurse she would have wanted working beside her at the Waverley.

Exactly the kind of man you'd want in your life, too, if he wasn't so completely unreliable with women, a small voice whispered in her head, and she squashed the thought immediately.

'Clear!' Eli said, taking the paddles from her and placing them on either side of Mr Finlay's thin chest, and immediately Brontë sat back on her heels so she would not be subjected to a two hundred joules shock herself.

Mr Finlay's back arched slightly on the floor as the electricity coursed through him, and Eli and Brontë stared at the heart monitor. No change.

'Three hundred joules,' Eli ordered.

Swiftly Brontë changed the voltage on the defibrillator.

'Three hundred joules,' she confirmed.

'Clear!' Eli exclaimed, and again Brontë sat back, but though Mr Finlay's body arched again, the heart monitor didn't change.

'Three hundred and sixty joules,' Eli said, 'and get me the epinephrine.'

Brontë nodded. Epinephrine could help the heart be more receptive to jolts of electricity and, if Mr Finlay's heart wasn't being kick-started into a regular rhythm by the three hundred and sixty joules alone, it was the only thing they had left to try.

Anxiously, she watched the heart monitor as Eli administered the three hundred and sixty joules, but there was no alteration, not even the slightest suspicion of one, and she handed him the epinephrine. Quickly, he injected it, applied the paddles again, and from then on he swung into a grim routine. Drug...shock...drug...shock, with the only sound being that of kettles being boiled in the kitchen.

How long had they been doing this? Brontë wondered as she felt the minutes tick by. How long could they continue doing it before they would have to concede Mr Finlay was not going to come back?

'I don't give up easily, Brontë,' Eli muttered as though he'd read her mind. 'Paddles again.'

Obediently, Brontë handed them to him and, as Eli placed them on either side of Mr Finlay's chest, and the electric shock ran through him, the heart monitor's erratic recordings suddenly changed. Miraculously, they had a pattern. It was much too slow, much too deep, but at least it was regular.

'Pulse?' Eli demanded.

'Weak and slow, but there,' Brontë replied.

'Okay, we go,' Eli declared, and she nodded.

They might have got Mr Finlay back, but his heart could return to VF at any minute. He needed A and E, but first they would have to negotiate three flights of stairs, and Mr Finlay was a big man. A very big man.

'How strong is your back?' Brontë asked as Eli stood, and Mrs Finlay appeared carrying an armful of blankets, and two flasks.

'I was going to ask you the same thing,' Eli replied wryly. 'Thank heavens for the carry-chair. Trying to get him down those stairs on a stretcher would have been a nightmare.'

It wasn't much easier with the carry-chair, Brontë decided. By the time they'd reached the ground floor she was breathless, and sweaty, and her arms and shoulders felt as though they had been pulled out of their sockets.

'Blue this one in, Brontë,' Eli ordered, as he climbed in beside Mr Finlay and his wife at the back of the ambulance. 'Up the siren to max, and step on it!'

She did, but it wasn't an easy ride. According to their sat nav, the quickest way to the hospital was via some of Edinburgh's back roads, but those streets also contained a hazard she hadn't been prepared for.

'I'm sorry—so sorry,' she shouted over her shoulder as she heard Eli swear when the ambulance lurched jerkily to one side yet again. 'If I could avoid these wretched speed bumps, I would, but I can't.'

'And if I had my way I'd strap every Edinburgh council-lor to a trolley, then put him in an ambulance and drive them over these damn things for ten minutes, and you can bet your life they'd have them all dug up before I could say Elijah Munroe!' he exclaimed.

Brontë could not help but agree with him, and nor could she restrain her sigh of relief when she saw the lights of the Pentland Infirmary shining through the dark in front of them. Their journey might only have taken ten minutes, but it had seemed like a lifetime.

'I hope Mr Finlay makes it,' she observed after the nurses and doctors had taken over from them, and whisked Mr Finlay and his wife away.

'We did our best,' Eli replied with a tired smile, 'and it's all we can do. Which reminds me,' he added. 'When we were coming down the stairs, I noticed—'

'I didn't always bend my knees,' she finished for him. 'Yes, I know. I'm out of practice lifting people.'

'It's not that,' he said. 'It's your boots.'

'I bought a new pair,' she protested. 'I went to Harper & Stolins this afternoon...' She glanced at her watch. 'Actually, yesterday afternoon now, and I bought a pair.'

'Those are not Safari boots,' he said firmly. 'You may well have bought them from Harper & Stolins but they are not Safari.'

'The Safari ones were too heavy,' she replied. 'The Wayfarer ones were lighter, more fashionable—'

'There's a reason for them being heavier,' he interrupted with great and obvious patience. 'It's to ensure you keep your toes.'

'Okay, all right.' She grimaced. 'So I bought the wrong boots, but must you always be so...so...'

'Right about everything?' he suggested with a smile.

'Smug,' she countered. 'Smug was the word I was searching for. I'll go back this afternoon and buy a pair of Safaris.'

'What time this afternoon?'

She had to think. Working nights was really throwing her awareness of time completely.

'I'll probably be sleeping until about two,' she replied, 'then I need to do some washing, and buy some food…. As tonight's late-night shopping, I'll probably go about eight o'clock.'

'Then I'll meet you outside Harper & Stolins at eight o'clock to make sure you get the right boots this time. And before you argue with me,' he added as she opened her mouth to do just that, 'I'm damned if I am going to have to live for the rest of my life with the knowledge that, because I didn't supervise you, you lost all your toes.'

'But—'

'Eight o'clock, Brontë.'

She gave in. 'Okay, I'll meet you outside the shop. Happy now?'

He was until they got back into the ambulance, and then she heard him groan.

'What's up?' she asked.

'That last call-out. It was a failure.'

'Mr Finlay?' She faltered. 'You mean… He's died?'

'I don't know,' Eli replied. 'It's one of the downsides of being a paramedic. Unless we specifically make enquiries, we never get to find out what's happened to the people we pick up.'

'Then what are you talking about?' she protested. 'We arrived at Holyrood Gate to find Mr Finlay wasn't breathing, you got his heart beating again, we've delivered him to A and E, so you've given him the best possible chance of survival. No way is that a failure.'

'It is if you look at the dashboard,' Eli declared. 'I hit the timer when we got the call-out, and hit it again when we arrived in Holyrood Gate, and I've only just checked it. Look at the reading, Brontë.'

She did, but it didn't help.

'I'm sorry, but I'm still not with you,' she said.

'Brontë, it was a cat-A, high-priority call. If you remember, an ambulance crew should arrive at a cat-A call-out in eight minutes. It doesn't matter what happens to the patient *after* we get there, just so long as we get there in eight minutes, and we took nine minutes.'

She gazed at him in disbelief. 'Then, you're saying…'

'If we had arrived at Holyrood Gate in eight minutes to discover Mr Finlay had been dead for two days, it would be counted as a success. If we arrived, as we did, in nine minutes, providing him with life-saving treatment, it's a failure.'

'But that's…' She thought about it, but thinking didn't make it any better. *'Nuts.'*

'Yup,' he agreed, wearily rubbing his hands over his face, 'and it's not just nuts. It also costs the station dearly because the more eight-minute targets we miss, the less money the government will give us to buy new vehicles, and employ more staff. Mr Finlay's call-out was a financial disaster for ED7.'

All the elation Brontë had felt in getting Mr Finlay safely to the Pentland drained away in an instant. She knew she couldn't possibly have got to Holyrood Gate any faster. No one could unless they'd had wings, and as she stared unhappily at Eli, she realised he suddenly looked every one of his thirty-eight years.

'How do you stand this?' she asked. 'The stupid rules, the petty restrictions?'

'Because…' He drew in a deep breath, then shook his head awkwardly. 'Hell, but this is going to sound so pretentious. I might hate the bureaucracy, the reducing of patients to numbers instead of people with feelings, hopes and dreams, but… Every once in a while I make a difference. Every once in a while my being there can pull someone through who wouldn't otherwise survive, and on those occasions…'

'It's the best job in the world,' she said, and he smiled, a weary, sad smile.

'That's about it.'

It was how she'd used to feel in A and E, she remembered. The rush of adrenaline when they'd been able to resuscitate someone, the buzz in the department when everything went well. Yes, there were downsides. The consultants who could be rude and overbearing, the times when they couldn't save someone, but she missed it, she missed it so much.

'Coffee,' she said firmly. 'I think we both need coffee, and I want the biggest, stickiest, sugar-covered doughnut Tony's can supply.'

'Not a hamburger?' Eli said, his blue eyes crinkling, and she knew the effort it had taken him to make that small joke, and gave him a mock hard stare.

'A doughnut, Mr Munroe.'

'Then hit the road, O'Brian,' he replied, 'and don't spare the horses.'

She didn't. She reached the café in record time but, when Eli had gone to get their food and drinks, she stared morosely out of the ambulance.

How in the world had she ever believed she could do this job? It had been a mistake even to have applied for it. She should have looked into the details more fully, paid more attention to what her duties would be, but she had been so desperate for a job, any job.

And you wanted something which would keep you connected, however tenuously, to nursing, her mind whispered, and she sighed.

Not once since she'd started working at the station had she ever taken out her notebook because it was the patients who interested her, they always had. Nursing was where her heart lay and, though Eli seemed to think she could retrain to be a paramedic, unless she could get over her fear of crowds it just wasn't an option, and that left her...

Nowhere, she thought with an even deeper sigh. Absolutely nowhere.

'One-a cappuccino, one-a doughnut,' Eli announced with a flourish as he opened the cab door.

'You're a lifesaver,' she replied, forcing a smile to her lips, but he wasn't fooled for a second.

'Let it go, Brontë,' he said gently. 'Take a tip from one who knows. The petty restrictions, the rules and regulations, let them go and concentrate on the fact we got Mr Finlay to hospital because, if you don't, it eats away at you, makes you cynical, bitter.'

'I know,' she murmured, 'but...' She shook her head. 'I don't think I'm cut out for this job.'

'I don't think you are either,' he agreed, and she glowered at him.

'Couldn't you at least *pretend* to think I might be?' she exclaimed. 'Sheesh, but you really know how to dent a woman's self-esteem, don't you?'

'Would you rather I'd lied?' he asked, and she bit her lip.

'No, but you could have glossed it up a bit,' she pointed out. 'You could have said, "Well, Brontë, I think you're really good at this job, but I just know you'd be even better doing something else."'

He grinned. 'Yeah, but the big question is, would you have bought it if I'd said that?'

She wouldn't, but it was singularly depressing to know this was the second job she'd failed at within the space of a year.

'If you decide this isn't right for you,' he continued as she took a morose bite out of her doughnut, 'how about retraining to become a paediatrics nurse, or something in surgical?'

'I could, except...' She grimaced slightly. 'I don't mind kids, but nursing them all the time... And as for surgical... There wouldn't be the same buzz I used to get from A and E.'

'Brontë—'

'Anyway, it's not your problem, is it?' she said brightly. 'So let's talk about something else.'

She was right, he realised, it wasn't his problem so why did he feel so concerned? What she did, where she went after the end of this week, was surely her own business, and it shouldn't matter to him what decision she made, and yet, to his acute annoyance, he discovered it did.

Protective. Hell but he had that feeling again, and it didn't make any sense. He had never once felt protective of any his ex-girlfriends, so why in the world was he feeling it now about a woman he barely knew?

Because she's had such a rotten time this past year, he told himself. She's been stabbed, she suffers from panic attacks, and she's going to be out of a job because she sure as heck can't do an assessor's one. Only a complete louse wouldn't feel sorry for her.

Except feeling sorry isn't the same as feeling protective.

'Why are you glowering at me?'

'Glowering?' he repeated blankly, and saw Brontë shake her head.

'You're glowering at me, like I've rained on your parade or something, so what have I done wrong now?'

No way was he going to tell her his thoughts, and so he said the first thing that came into his head.

'Why Brontë?'

'Why Brontë, what?' she asked, taking a sip of her coffee.

'No, I meant how did you get your Christian name?'

'Oh, that's easy,' she replied. 'My parents both lecture in, and are fanatical fans of, English nineteenth-century literature, so I got stuck with Brontë. Actually, in the greater scheme of things, I was lucky. My big brother got landed with Byron, and my little sister with Rossetti.'

'And are your brother and sister medics like you?'

'Oh, heavens, no.' She laughed. 'Byron is an investment banker, and Rossetti's a criminal lawyer.'

His eyebrows rose. 'Serious high-flyers.'

'Yup, I'm the dummkopf of the family,' she replied, and saw a flash of unexpected irritation cross his face.

'Why do you think you're the dummkopf?' he demanded.

'Because I am in comparison to them,' she replied. 'Look, it's no big deal,' she continued, as he opened his mouth, clearly intending to interrupt, 'we can't all be high-flyers and I don't have a problem with it. Do you have any brothers or sisters?'

'No.'

An oddly shuttered look had suddenly appeared on his face. A look which suggested she had inadvertently strayed into an area he considered very much off limits, and she wished she hadn't asked, except it was hardly a controversial question, and yet it appeared it was.

'Good coffee,' she said awkwardly. 'Good doughnut, too.'

'Maybe I'll tempt you into trying one of Tony's hamburgers one night,' he said, clearly deeply relieved to be talking about something else. 'Better yet, maybe you'll tell me about the blond who did such a number on you that you've given up dating permanently.'

She rolled her eyes.

'Don't you *ever* give up?' she exclaimed.

'Nope.'

Which would teach her the folly of embellishing a lie, she thought ruefully. There wasn't a blond, never had been unless she counted the fair-haired medical student she'd dated for a few weeks when she was training to be a nurse, but how to explain what she didn't fully understand herself. That as far as men were concerned she seemed to have an invisible sticker on her forehead saying, *This one's a mug*. Eli knowing she was a fruit cake when it came to encountering drunken gangs was one thing, her admitting to him she was also the world's biggest all-time loser in the game of love was something else entirely.

'Next question, please,' she said firmly.

'Quit stalling, O'Brian,' he pressed. 'Tell me.'

She wouldn't have told him anything, but he was smiling that smile at her again. The 'tell me all your troubles' smile, the 'you can trust me' smile, and she gazed heavenwards with frustration.

'Look, if I tell you, will you quit harassing me?' she demanded, and when he nodded, she took a deep breath. 'It's got nothing to do with any blond. I just have such lousy taste in men I thought, Why keep on getting hurt, why not just concede defeat, and give up on dating completely.'

A frown appeared in his blue eyes. 'You mean, you attract men who hurt you physically?'

'No, I don't mean that,' she said irritably.

'Then you attract psychos, weirdos?'

'You mean like the loony tune I'm currently sitting next to?' she said in exasperation. 'No, I don't mean that either. It's just…every man I've ever dated… It always starts off okay, and then…' She shrugged. 'I guess I don't see the warning signs quickly enough that the men I get involved with aren't right for me.'

'Why?'

'I don't *know*. Look, you asked me,' she continued quickly as Eli opened his mouth clearly intending to push it, 'and I've answered your question. *End of discussion.*'

Not for Eli it wasn't, she realised as he waved the remains of his hamburger pointedly at her.

'Okay, as I see it,' he declared, 'you're making two fundamental mistakes here. First, you're choosing the wrong men to date.'

'Well, duh,' she replied. 'I wonder why I didn't think of

that. *Of course* I'm choosing the wrong men to date, but I don't deliberately set out to fall in love with men who will break my heart. I just seem to end up with them.'

'And that's your second mistake,' Eli observed. 'You're looking for *lurve*, for the happy-ever-after ending, and there's no such thing.'

She blinked. 'You don't believe there's any such thing as love?'

'Of course there isn't,' he replied, taking a large gulp of his coffee. 'All that hearts and flowers stuff, the mushy sentimental ballads and films… It all boils down to sex.'

'But—'

'Brontë, the quicker you wake up and face reality, the less chance you'll have of being hurt,' he insisted. 'Forget about love, forget about happy-ever-afters. Relationships between men and women all come down to one thing. What the sex is like. If the sex is mediocre, you cut your losses. If the sex is okay, you stick around for a bit because okay sex is better than no sex at all, and if the sex is phenomenal you enjoy it while you can, and then move on. It's what grown-up, realistic men and women do.'

'No, you're wrong, so wrong,' she argued back. 'There *is* love in this world. Yes, there's a lot of suffering, a lot of pain, but I truly believe there are people out there caring for one another, loving one another. If I didn't believe that—if I just accepted, as you seem to, that everyone just looks after themselves—what kind of world would we have?'

Eli shook his head impatiently.

'You're confusing two completely different issues here,' he declared. 'I'm not saying you walk on by if someone's in trouble, or ignore another human being's suffering. There are a lot of things I care passionately about. Injustice, inequality, bigotry—'

'But not love?' she interrupted.

'No, not love,' he said firmly, and she sighed in defeat.

'Could any two people possibly be more incompatible?' she observed. 'More poles apart in what they think, believe?'

'Doubt it,' he replied.

There didn't seem anything left to say, and, as Brontë stared down at the remains of her doughnut, it somehow didn't seem nearly as appealing as it had earlier.

'I think I've had enough of this,' she said, putting what was left of her doughnut back into its paper bag.

'I'm actually not very hungry tonight either,' Eli murmured, gazing down at his hamburger without enthusiasm.

'Back to the station, to wait for a call-out?' she suggested.

'Best thing,' he agreed. 'Except you'd better get rid of that icing sugar on your cheek first. No, the other cheek,' he continued impatiently as she put her hand up to her left cheek. 'Here, let me.'

She didn't get the chance to tell him she wasn't an idiot, that she could manage perfectly well on her own, thank you very much. He had already begun brushing the icing sugar from her cheek. Brushing it matter-of-factly at first, and then the pressure of his fingers suddenly changed. His touch became feather-light, almost caressing, and she forgot to breathe, forgot to do anything, but stare back at him. He hadn't moved closer to her, she could swear he hadn't, and yet he seemed so much nearer, the cabin so much smaller, and, when his fingers slid slowly down her cheek, and cupped her chin, she swallowed hard.

'Eli....'

She couldn't say anything else, and he didn't say anything at all. He just held her chin in his hand, his blue eyes fixed on her, so dark, so very dark in the light from the street lamp, and she could hear his breathing, could hear her own erratic breath in the silence, could feel a slow spiralling heat growing deep within her, and slowly she reached up and covered his hand with her own.

His fingers were warm, much warmer than hers, and she shivered involuntarily, saw his lips part, knew her own had, too, and she felt herself leaning towards him, saw he was leaning towards her in return, and then, suddenly, without warning, he wasn't holding her chin any more, and she was looking shakily out of the window, not sure whether it had been her, or him, who had moved first, or if they had moved in unison, but it was definitely Eli who spoke first, and his voice, when he did, sounded strained, husky.

'We'd better get back to the station.'

She nodded, or at least she thought she nodded, and with her heart still jumping erratically in her chest, she switched on the ignition and hoped to heaven he couldn't see just how much her hands were trembling as she drove away.

CHAPTER FOUR

Thursday, 7:55 p.m.

SHE should have arranged to meet Eli earlier, Brontë thought as she stamped her feet, and blew on her fingers to try to restore some heat to them, as an icy wind swirled around Cockburn Street. Better yet, she should have told him at the end of their shift this morning that she'd suddenly remembered something absolutely vital she had to do, and couldn't meet him at all.

Not that they'd exactly been talking when they'd finished work, she remembered ruefully. He'd seemed as anxious to get away as she had, which meant this shopping trip was going to be awkward, and uncomfortable, and she should have stayed home.

'Oh, stop it, Brontë,' she muttered to herself. 'It's not like this is a date. You've both agreed you're completely incompatible, and him coming on this shopping trip is more a colleague-to-colleague advisory type thing.'

Which doesn't explain why you've washed your hair, and put on your favourite knee-length brown leather boots, and equally favourite racing green coat with the faux-fur-trimmed hood.

Well, my hair needed a wash, she defensively told her reflection in the large window of Harper & Stolins, and as for my clothes… Only an idiot wouldn't have wrapped up warmly when it definitely felt like snow.

Yeah, right, Brontë, a little voice laughed as she tried in vain to smooth down her fringe which was most definitely sticking up. *So it's got nothing to do with what happened earlier this morning, then?*

Oh, my word, but that had been something else, Brontë thought, feeling a flutter of heat in her stomach as she remembered. When he'd touched her cheek, when their eyes had met, and time had seemed to disappear… She'd been so certain he was going to kiss her, had so wanted him to kiss her, and she closed her eyes, to relive the memory, and let out a tiny yelp when a hand clasped her shoulder.

'Will you stop *doing* that?' She gasped, clutching at her chest as she whirled round to see Eli standing behind her.

'I thought it was just dark cemeteries which spooked you,' he protested, 'not well-lit streets in Edinburgh.'

Everything about you spooks me, she wanted to reply, but she didn't.

'Yeah, well, wear shoes with heavier soles next time,' she said instead.

In fact, change absolutely everything you're wearing, she thought as her gaze took in his appearance. Eli dressed in his paramedic cargo trousers, and high-visibility jacket, might be enough to set most feminine hearts aflutter, but Eli wearing a pair of hip-hugging denims, a blue-and-white open-necked shirt and an old black leather jacket was guaranteed to give every woman a cardiac arrest. A fact that was all too obvious from the number of women who were giving him second glances as they walked by.

'So,' he said, 'are you ready for the big boots expedition?'

Was it her imagination or did he seem just a little bit uncomfortable, a little unsure, almost as though he wished he was anywhere but here?

'Look, you don't have to do this,' she said quickly. 'I promise faithfully I'll buy the correct boots this time, so you don't need to babysit me.'

'Hey, it's no problem,' he insisted. 'And I have to safe-guard your toes, remember?'

She laughed, and he did, too, and if his laughter sounded slightly strained to her ears, she decided it was probably just because he was as cold as she was.

'Okay,' she said, 'let's get on with it, shall we?'

Getting on with it, however, looked as though it might take considerably longer than she'd anticipated. They were cer-tainly whisked instantly through to the seating area when they entered Harper & Stolins, and there were assistants aplenty, but unfortunately each and every one of them appeared to want to talk to Eli. Of course, that was probably because all of them were women, Brontë thought wryly, but feeling like a spare parcel abandoned at a sorting office was not how she had envisaged spending her boot-buying expedition.

'Any chance of some service here?' she said eventually to one of the girls who was hovering on the outskirts of Eli's fan club.

'Sorry,' the girl declared, looking as though she actually meant it, 'but Eli's a very popular customer.'

'So I see.' Brontë sighed. 'I'm looking for a pair of Safari boots, size five.'

The girl was back within minutes, clutching a pair, and it was only when Brontë put them on she realised the folly of wearing a skirt when you were trying on safety boots.

'What's wrong?' Eli asked as he joined her beside the mirror, and saw her rueful expression.

'Not exactly flattering, are they?' she replied, looking down at her feet. 'In fact, I look like I'm auditioning for clown of the year.'

'They're not supposed to be flattering,' Eli observed. 'They're supposed to keep your toes in one piece.'

'I know, but…' She sighed as she lifted one foot. 'I should have worn trousers.'

'Not for me you shouldn't. It's nice to see you have legs.'

And he was staring at them. Staring at them in a quite blatant way, and she suddenly felt completely exposed, which was crazy because she walked around Edinburgh in skirts all the time, and had never once felt vulnerable.

'Of course I have legs,' she replied in a rush, horribly aware her cheeks were darkening. 'Everyone has legs. Unless they've lost them due to some accident, or were born that way, of course, in which case they won't but, generally, normally, most people have legs.'

And I'm babbling, she thought, babbling like an idiot, but I wish I'd worn trousers because he's still staring at my legs and my knees are too chunky, and my calves aren't exactly model-girl slim, and Eli likes girls with impossibly long legs, not that I give a damn about that, but…

'Everyone might have legs,' he said, 'but not everyone has great ones like you.'

He thought she had good legs. No, correct that. He thought she had *great* legs, and he was still looking at them, making her feel even more self-conscious.

'Do we have a sale?' the assistant asked, glancing from Brontë to Eli, then back again.

'I think so, yes,' Brontë replied. 'I mean they fit, and they're Safaris, so…'

She wished Eli would say something, anything, and what was worse was two of the assistants were nudging each other, and giggling, and she didn't know why they were giggling.

'These boots are the right ones, aren't they, Eli?' she continued pointedly. 'The ones you wanted me to buy?'

He blinked, then nodded. 'Absolutely. Definitely.'

'Well, that's my footwear sorted out for tonight,' she said

far too brightly as she sat down, feeling considerably flustered. 'Problem solved, mission accomplished.'

'So, what now?' he asked as she slipped into her knee-length boots, and headed for the till, clutching the Safaris.

'Now?' she repeated. 'Well, I guess once I've paid for the boots I go home, and you go and do whatever you were planning on doing before we clock on in a couple of hours.'

'You mean I don't even get to share a celebratory dinner with you?' he protested after she'd settled up with the cashier, and he followed her out onto the street. 'I've come all the way here from my warm and cosy flat in Lauriston Place to give you the benefit of my not-inconsiderable advice, and now it's snowing, and I don't even get something to eat?'

He wanted to prolong this nondate? He wanted to go somewhere else with her? She would have thought he would have been anxious to get away, to do something else, see someone else, and yet he clearly wasn't.

Go home, Brontë. Thank him for his kindness, and go home where it's safe.

Except he was right about the snow. Little flakes were beginning to whirl about in the wind, and settle on the pavement, and he hadn't needed to come and help her, even if she hadn't really needed any help. All she'd needed was to concede defeat, forget about fashion and style, and accept she had to wear a pair of boots which made her feet look like a penguin's.

'Dinner would be nice,' she admitted. 'But I live on the south side of Edinburgh so I wouldn't have a clue where to go round here.'

'The Black Bull in the High Street,' he announced. 'It's my favourite restaurant. They might not make coffee quite as good as Tony's, but they do make a mean Hungarian stroganoff and poached salmon to die for.'

And he was obviously as equally well known in the Black Bull as he was in Harper & Stolins, Brontë thought drily, when a beaming waitress ushered them towards a table by the roaring log fire, and an equally attentive waitress quickly took their orders. A stroganoff for Eli, and poached salmon for her.

'Do you know every single woman in Edinburgh?' Brontë asked as she shrugged off her coat, and held her hands out to the fire. 'And I'm emphasising the word *single* here.'

'Can I help it if I'm a popular guy?' Eli answered, and, despite herself, Brontë laughed.

'It's nice here,' she said, her eyes taking in the old oak panelling, the wheelback chairs, chintz curtains, and pictures of Old Edinburgh. 'Very cosy, and atmospheric. Though I'm surprised you like it. I'd have pegged you as more a minimalist, modern sort of a guy.'

'Now, what did I tell you about the dangers of taking me at face value?' he teased and, when she laughed again, he nodded approvingly. 'You don't do that often enough. Laugh, I mean. I wonder why that is?'

'Maybe I just take things more seriously than you do,' she replied. 'Or, maybe this past year has forced me to be more serious.'

To her surprise, Eli reached out, and covered one of her hands with his.

'Try not to remember it,' he said gently. 'Try not to look back, but look forward instead.'

Which was easy for him to say, Brontë thought wistfully as she stared down at his strong, capable fingers. He knew exactly what his future was, whereas she didn't even know what she would be doing next week.

'By the way, I think I've figured out why you're having such problems with men,' Eli continued, releasing her hand as the waitress placed their orders in front of them.

'I thought we'd already worked that one out,' she protested, trying not to mind that his hand was no longer covering hers.

'It's because I'm a lousy picker, and I believe in love which, according to you, doesn't exist.'

'Well, those are certainly issues, but I think they're part of a much bigger problem. How old is your brother?'

'Byron?' she said, bewildered by his unexpected change in conversation. 'He's thirty-six.'

'And your sister, Rossetti?'

'She's twenty-eight, but…' She frowned at him. 'Sorry, but I thought you were going to explain why I have such bad luck with men, but now you're talking about my family, so is there a reason behind your questions, or are you just going off at a tangent?'

He sighed pointedly. 'Could you just bear with me here for one minute, Brontë. This is important. How old are you?'

'Thirty-five, but I don't see—'

'You've got middle-child syndrome.'

'I've got what?' she said, starting to laugh, but he looked so perfectly serious she stopped. 'Okay, enlighten me. What's middle-child syndrome?'

He took a bite of his stroganoff, then sat back in his seat.

'The first child in a family is always the most anticipated and exciting for the parent so it's put on a pedestal, applauded for everything it does, and made a big fuss of. That's your brother, Byron. The baby of the family basks in the sentimentality of being the last child, so it's basically spoiled rotten. That's your sister, Rossetti.'

'And me?' she said, curious in spite of herself as she ate some of her poached salmon and found it to be every bit as good as he'd promised.

'Well, you… You were just there. Never getting the same praise as your brother and sister because having been through the toddler stages with Byron, your parents just expected you to learn how to do the same things he had, and Rossetti would be completely indulged because they knew she was going to be their last child. You were stuck in the middle, overlooked a lot of the time, so you grew up to suffer from severe low self-esteem.'

'I suspect your psychology is a bit skewed,' she observed uncomfortably, and he shook his head as he took a sip of water.

'Nope, it's pretty well documented.'

'But I don't feel inferior to my brother and sister.'

'*I'm the dummkopf of the family.* That's what you said,' he declared, 'and it bothered me—it bothered me a lot—that you should think being a nurse made you inferior to them.'

She wanted to tell Eli he was wrong, that she didn't feel at all inferior to Byron or Rossetti, but she suddenly realised she couldn't. It was hard not to feel inferior when her brother would telephone to say he was heading off to Hong Kong, or New York, or Tokyo, and it had been even harder to feel genuinely happy for Rossetti when their parents had bought her a plushy, three-bedroom flat while she was still living in rented accommodation.

'Okay, so maybe I do feel a little inferior to them,' she conceded, realising Eli was waiting for an answer. 'In fact, if I'm going to be completely honest, there were times, when I was growing up, and Byron won yet another collection of school prizes, and Rossetti appeared never to do anything wrong in my parents' eyes, I did wish I belonged to another family.'

'Knew it!' Eli exclaimed triumphantly.

'*But...*' Brontë continued determinedly. 'Every child feels inferior to its siblings at one time or another. I bet you did, too. I bet there were times when you thought, "Oh, to have been born into a different household, to some other family."'

'In my case, I would have been happy to have belonged to any family,' he murmured.

His face had that shuttered look again, she noticed. The look it always assumed when she strayed too far into something he clearly considered very personal, and she ate some more of her salmon, then slowly put down her knife and fork.

'Sounds like you had a rough childhood.'

'Water under the bridge now,' he said dismissively, but she sensed it wasn't, not for him.

'Eli—'

'Anyway, we're talking about you,' he interrupted, 'not me.'

So back off, Brontë. That's what he was saying. *Back off, keep out and don't probe.*

'Okay, if I accept you're right about me suffering from middle-child syndrome—which I don't,' she declared, seeing him roll his eyes as she picked up her knife and fork again, 'I fail to see how being a middle child explains my lousy track record with men.'

'It's obvious,' he said, attacking his stroganoff impatiently. 'If you're a middle child, with low self-esteem, that, in turn, makes you an easy target for fundamentally weak men who will walk all over you. You should be looking for a man who is self-confident, a man who is easy in his own skin.'

Like you, her heart whispered, and unconsciously she shook her head.

'Which is fine, in principle,' she argued back, 'but, surprising though it may be to you, even in the twenty-first century women don't tend to do the choosing, and if we see an example of the alpha male you seem to be describing there's precious few women who would go up to such a man, and ask *him* out.'

'But—'

'Eli, alpha men gravitate towards alpha women,' she continued, 'so they are not going to be asking someone like me out.'

A flash of anger appeared in his blue eyes.

'What do you mean, "someone like you"?' he said irritably. 'What's wrong with you?'

'Look at me, Eli.'

'I *am* looking,' he protested.

'No, not like that,' she replied with exasperation. 'Look at me the way a man looks at a woman he's scoping out.'

'Yeah, right,' he said wryly, 'and like I want all my teeth knocked out.'

'I'll give you a pass on this one, I promise,' she insisted, 'just look at me.'

Obediently, he put down his knife and fork, steepled his fingers together and leant forward.

'Okay, I'm looking.'

And, dear heavens, he was, she thought, feeling a flood of heat surge across her cheeks as his gaze swept over her figure, then up to her face, lingering for an instant on her lips, and then returned to her eyes. That look would have melted a polar ice cap, and as for her... Thank heavens she was sitting so close to the fire, because if she hadn't been she didn't know how on earth she would have explained why she not only felt ablaze, but also looked it.

'Okay, tell me what you see?' she managed to ask.

No way on this earth was he going to tell her what he saw, he thought as he moved uncomfortably in his seat, all too aware of a painful tightness in his groin. No way was he going to say he saw a woman who wasn't even pretty, far less beautiful. A woman whose gold-flecked brown hair was currently sticking out at a wild angle, and whose nose was chapped and red at the tip because of the cold weather they'd been having. A woman who, for some insane, inexplicable reason he still wanted to lean forward and kiss.

She'd think he was crazy. *He* thought he was crazy, and he had done so ever since last night when, if she hadn't moved away—or maybe he did first, he honestly couldn't remember now—he would have kissed her for sure, and that would have been bad, seriously bad.

'I see…' He cleared his throat. 'I see a young woman with a very winning personality.'

'Oh, wonderful.' Brontë groaned. 'That's exactly what every woman wants to hear. *Not.* Why don't you just offer me a paper bag to wear over my head the next time I go out?'

'Look, I phrased that wrongly,' he said quickly. 'What I meant—'

'It's okay, it's all right,' she said dismissively. 'I asked for your opinion, and you've given it. I know I'm not an alpha woman.' She thought about it, and frowned. 'Actually, I'm probably not even a gamma woman if there is such a thing, because I bet your first thought when you saw me on Monday night was, Ordinary, boring.'

It had been, he remembered. It had been exactly what he'd thought, and he'd been so wrong, so very wrong, just as he had been wrong to prolong their meeting after she'd bought her boots. Having almost made a complete fool of himself in Harpers & Stolins, by staring at her legs—and she had very good legs, he remembered, forcing himself not to look down and check them out again—he should simply have waved her farewell, and gone home, instead of urging her to spend more time in his company.

So why did you?

Because I wanted to prove to myself that last night—this morning—had been a temporary aberration, he thought ruefully. I wanted to see her outside of the station environment, so I'd realise she's just another woman, not in any way different or special, but the trouble is she *is* different and I don't know why.

'You're taking too long to answer, Eli,' she pointed out, and he felt a tide of heat creep up the back of his neck.

'Of course I didn't think you were boring,' he lied, and she shook her head.

'Yes, you did, and that's what I am. Brontë O'Brian. Memorable only because of my name, so thanks for your advice about dating only superconfident alpha men but, trust me, it ain't going to happen.'

'What about dating men who are all screwed up?' he said before he could stop himself, and Brontë laughed.

'Men like you, you mean?' she replied.

The minute the words were out of her mouth, she wished them back. What she'd said... It sounded almost—hell, it sounded *exactly*—as though she was hitting on him, and she hadn't intended to do that, and she opened her mouth to say something flippant, light, but the words died in her throat.

He had reached out and taken one of her hands in his, and was staring down at it, his face a little wry.

'I certainly feel completely screwed up at the moment,' he murmured.

'Do you?' she said faintly, and he nodded.

'You see, the trouble is...' He met her gaze. 'I just can't figure you out at all.'

'I thought...' Oh, my heavens, but he was stroking the palm of her hand with his thumb, and she was having difficulty thinking, far less speaking. 'I thought we'd established I was easy to read. That I'm suffering from middle-child syndrome, and I'm ordinary and boring.'

'You're definitely suffering from middle-child syndrome, but you're anything but ordinary and boring. You're...' A rueful smile appeared in his blue eyes. 'You're one of a kind, Brontë O'Brian.'

One of a kind. Did that mean what she thought—hoped—it meant? Did it mean he found her desirable, not ordinary and boring at all, but actually desirable? She knew she should say something, but she didn't know what to say, didn't want to mess it up, and she cleared her throat, only to pause.

A log had shifted in the grate beside her, sending a shower of snapping, crackling sparks spiralling up into the chimney, but it wasn't that which had caught her attention. It was the muffled, feminine laughter behind her and, as she glanced over her shoulder and saw the knowing smile on the face of one of the waitresses, she realised something she should have seen before. Something she must have been blind not to have been aware of, and a twist of pain tore through her.

Eli was flirting with her. Not because it meant anything, not because he was interested in her, but simply because he could, and she, like a poor sap, was falling for it, falling for his charm, just as all the other women in his life had. He was playing with her, and she had never played games when it came to relationships. For her it had always been all or nothing, and with Eli she knew as surely as she knew anything that if she didn't stop this right now it would simply lead to a broken heart, and she couldn't go that way, just couldn't.

Blindly, she pulled her hand out of his, and reached for her coat.

'I…I have to go,' she said through a throat so tight it hurt.

'But why?' he protested, confusion plain on his face. 'You haven't finished your meal—'

'I need… I have to go home to get changed,' she said, frantically searching under the table for her carrier bag from Harper & Stolins, desperate to get away from him.

'But, we're not on duty until ten-thirty,' Eli declared. 'We've another hour—'

'I need to shower as well,' Brontë said, looking everywhere but at him. 'I…I need to shower, and change, and get ready for tonight.'

She was already heading for the restaurant door and, without even counting them, Eli pressed some notes into the waitress's hand, and hurried after her.

'Brontë, what's wrong?' he demanded when he caught up with her in the street.

'Nothing…absolutely nothing,' she said with forced brightness. 'Thank you for the help with the boots, and the lovely meal. I'll see you tonight.'

'But, Brontë—'

Don't come after me, she prayed, as she walked quickly away from him down the High Street, the sound of her feet muffled by the now lying snow. *Please, please, don't come after me,* her heart cried as she dashed a hand across her cheeks, despising herself for her weakness and stupidity.

To her relief he didn't. To her relief, no familiar voice called her name, no firm hand grasped her shoulder, but it didn't help. She might be able to lose herself amongst the other late-night shoppers who were thronging the street, but she couldn't shut out the mocking little voice in her head.

The little voice that whispered, *Fool, Brontë. You are such a fool.*

Eli rotated his shoulders wearily as Brontë drove carefully down Johnstone Terrace towards Stables Road. An RTC, Dispatch had said, and it wasn't the first such accident they'd been called out to tonight. In fact, from the minute they'd clocked on at ten-thirty, they'd scarcely had a moment's rest, not even for their customary coffee break. The now deeply lying snow, coupled with inexperienced city drivers unused to driving in such conditions, had meant accident after accident, and ED7's resources had been stretched to breaking point.

'The police are here,' Brontë observed as a flashing light suddenly appeared in the dark in front of them. 'Must be a serious one.'

It looked it, even from a distance and, when they got nearer, it looked even worse. The car had clearly skidded right across the road, but then it had hit a wall, and brought part of the wall down on top of it.

'I'm afraid the driver looks in a pretty bad way,' one of the policemen declared when Brontë and Eli walked towards him. 'According to her ID, her name is Katie Lee, aged twenty.'

And she hadn't been wearing a seat belt, Eli thought as he stared at the car. He could see the distinctive ringed crack on the windscreen which meant the young woman had 'bullseyed' it when her car had hit the wall, and there were tiny spots of blood and bits of hair embedded in the glass. Why didn't people learn—why did they never seem to learn?

'Dear heavens, the whole front of the bonnet is completely crushed,' Brontë whispered.

He could hear the shock in her voice, the appalled horror, but then she would only ever have seen people who had been brought in to A and E by ambulance, and not the situations they had come out of, as he always did.

'Watch out for broken glass, and bits of metal,' he replied, 'and if you see any oil, let me know. We don't want to be inside something that might go up like a fireball.'

'Right,' she said faintly. She glanced up at him. 'I'm okay, honestly I am. It's just…'

'The first bad RTC is always a bit of a shock.' He nodded. 'I threw up after my first one.'

She managed a smile but, when he smiled back, she looked away quickly and he bit his lip.

She'd scarcely said a word to him all night, and it wasn't simply because they'd been run off their feet. She was clearly edgy and uncomfortable in his company, and it was all his fault.

Why in the world had he virtually asked her whether she would consider dating him, he wondered, as he leant into the driver's seat to take the young woman's pulse, and heard the mobile phone lying on the car floor begin to ring. He still didn't know why he'd said it. The words had just come out, completely without warning, so thank heavens Brontë had taken the initiative, and ended the conversation. If she'd said, 'Okay, Eli, where do you want to go on this date?' he would have been in severe trouble because he'd made his no-dating pledge, and it still had a month to run.

Oh, get outta here, Eli, his mind laughed. *That isn't what's freaking you out. What's freaking you out is that for the first*

*time in your life you feel all at sea with a woman, and it's
scaring you half to death.*

'Katie…Katie, can you hear me?' Brontë said as she leant
in through the broken window of the passenger door.

'My legs…my legs hurt so much, and my chest…' The
young woman groaned as she tried to take a breath. 'It's like
there's a big, heavy weight on it.'

'Pulse weak, BP falling,' Eli muttered as he swiftly
wrapped a cervical collar round the young woman's neck
to support it before they could attempt to take her out of the
car. 'Looks like compound fractures tib and fib and possible
pelvis fracture to me.'

It would have been Brontë's initial assessment, too, plus
she strongly suspected severe internal injuries.

'Pethidine?' she suggested, and Eli nodded.

'Haemaccel drip, too,' he added. 'Is the heart monitor good
to go?'

'Just about,' Brontë murmured. 'Okay, it's on.'

They both stared at the screen, then exchanged glances.
The young woman's heart rate was erratic, extremely erratic,
and the last thing they wanted, or needed, was her to go into
VF within the small confines of the car, or, even worse, to go
asystole. Asystole hearts couldn't be shocked. All they could
do, if that occurred, was perform CPR, and affix an Ambu
bag to try to keep the oxygen flowing to the young woman's
brain, but casualties who presented at A and E with asystole
rarely survived.

'Is there no way we can switch that off?' Brontë exclaimed
as the young woman's mobile phone began to ring again, and
she saw a message flash up on the display screen.

A message which read, 'Katie, can you call me? It's
Mum.'

'Try to ignore it,' Eli replied.

Brontë gritted her teeth, and tried her best, but it was hard.
Hard to see that message constantly flashing, and to know that

unless they got Katie to A and E quickly she might never be able to reply. Hard, too, she thought as she glanced over at Eli's lowered head as he swiftly inserted a drip, to persuade herself that the man working so closely beside her meant nothing to her, that he was simply a colleague, but she was going to do it. She was going to distance herself from him no matter what it took. She had to for her own self-preservation.

'How are we going to get her out of the car?' she said when she'd finished attaching an Ambu bag. 'So much of it is crushed. Should we call for the fire brigade?'

Eli frowned, then, as Katie Lee groaned, he clearly came to a decision.

'We can't afford to wait. Her BP's going through the floor, and I think she's bleeding internally.'

'But...'

'We get her out, Brontë.'

And they did, by the simple expedient of Eli taking most of the weight of the roof of the car upon himself as well as Katie's legs and torso.

'Your shoulders are going to be black and blue tomorrow,' Brontë observed, seeing Eli wince when he straightened up after they had safely carried Katie into the ambulance.

'Nothing I can't live with,' he replied dismissively. 'And getting her to A and E is much more important than me getting a couple of bruises.'

He meant that, she knew he did. Even in the short time she'd been working with him she'd seen he would always go that extra mile for the people who needed his professional skills, and yet he wouldn't go one step for the women in his life. Was it simply because he truly didn't believe in love, or was there something else? She wished she knew. She wished even more that she didn't care about the answer because not caring would have been much, much safer.

'I'll be glad when this shift is over,' she said after she

and Eli had taken the young woman to the Pentland. 'I'm shattered.'

'Me, too,' he replied. 'And yet, in a weird and horrible way, having to deal with all these accidents, fighting to keep people alive until we can get them to A and E… It's the sort of night we paramedics long for. Which—when you think about it—means we're either adrenaline junkies or must have hearts of stone.'

'I think it simply means if you've been trained to do difficult, complex procedures, the last thing you want is to be constantly presented with trivial ones,' Brontë said thoughtfully. 'I bet a plumber feels exactly the same. I bet he thinks, Wish I was out there fitting a challenging, state-of-the-art power shower system instead of unblocking yet another bogstandard sink.'

Eli stared at her in open-mouthed astonishment for a second, his eyes red-rimmed and shadowed with exhaustion, and then, to her surprise, he burst out laughing.

'Only you could think of that!' he exclaimed.

'But it's *true*,' Brontë insisted, and he laughed again.

'I know it is, but only you would say it out loud which is why I think I like…'

'Like what?' she asked, and saw him shake his head uncomfortably.

'Nothing. Not important.'

'But—'

'Isn't that Dr Carter?' he interrupted. 'Maybe she'll have some news for us about John.'

Helen Carter did, but it wasn't good.

'I'm really sorry, Eli,' she said unhappily. 'But it was Mr Duncan who did the rounds on Men's Medical this morning, and he created a bit of a stink about young John.'

'In other words, he kicked him out,' Eli declared with barely suppressed anger. 'He took one look at the boy's chart, refused to listen to any of the background information, and discharged him.'

'I think the words, "This is not a bed-and-breakfast establishment for down-and-outs" was used.' Dr Carter sighed. 'I did put a note on John's file, saying "exceptional circumstances"—'

'I'm sure you did, Helen,' Eli interrupted grimly, 'but Duncan's one of the old-school consultants, never does anything unless it's by the book. He just doesn't seem able to see that if we help people when they first present they'll need less medical attention in the future.'

'You did your best, Eli,' Dr Carter replied, her round face concerned.

'Yeah, well, it wasn't good enough this time, was it?'

And before Helen Carter could say anything else, he had walked away, and, with a quick glance of apology at Dr Carter, Brontë hurried after him.

'Eli, it wasn't your fault,' she said when she caught up with him in the street.

'And is that supposed to make me feel better?' he retorted. 'Peg *trusted* me, Brontë, and I failed her and the boy. Especially the boy.'

'At least you tried—'

'And a fat lot of use that did!' he snapped.

'Eli—'

'Just drive,' he said. 'I don't care where you go, but get me away from here because, if you don't, I swear I'll go back in there and find Duncan, and if I do…'

He didn't need to finish his sentence. Brontë waited only until he had snapped on his seat belt and she was off, driving down the Canongate, onwards past Abbey Mount, but, when she turned into Montrose Terrace, she heard him unclip his seat belt.

'I can't sit here,' he muttered. 'Stop the ambulance, Brontë. I need… I have to walk.'

Obediently, she drew up at the kerbside but, when he got out, and began walking up and down the pavement, his hands tight, balled fists at his side, she knew she couldn't simply sit there in the ambulance, watching him. No matter what he was, or what he had done, her heart bled for him. He had tried so hard to help John, had really cared about what happened to the boy, and she couldn't let him walk up and down the snow-covered pavement alone.

'Are you okay?' she asked tentatively as she approached him.

'What kind of damn fool question is that?' Eli exclaimed, then closed his eyes and, when he opened them, she could see regret there. 'I'm sorry, so sorry.' He gave an uneven laugh. 'Do you realise I've apologised to you more in the past four days than I have to anyone else in my whole life?'

'Maybe that's because you've never met anyone quite as irritating as me before,' she said, hoping to at least provoke a smile, but she didn't. 'Do you want to go and look for John? We could try Greyfriars. He might have gone back to Peg.'

'Didn't you hear what she said when we took him away on Tuesday?' he said morosely. 'She said, "I don't want to see you back here again, young feller."'

'Yes, but she meant it kindly,' Brontë replied, hating to see him looking so defeated. 'She meant she hoped he was going on to a better life.'

'He won't see it as such. He'll see it as an order not to go back to Greyfriars. He could be anywhere, Brontë, and trying to find him…' He shook his head. 'There are so many homeless people in Edinburgh.'

'Perhaps he'll go home,' Brontë said without much hope, but feeling she had to try to give Eli some. 'Or if he doesn't go home, maybe someone from one of the charities might pick him up, and he'll be okay.'

'Brontë, just what planet are you living on?' Eli exclaimed

angrily. 'He's more likely to become a crackhead, or a rent boy, than be *okay*.'

'I know—'

'You *don't*,' he replied, almost shouting at her now. 'You have no idea what it's like to be out on these streets, alone, and friendless. No comprehension of the temptations, the quick-fix drugs that are offered to you which you're only too happy to accept because they allow you an escape for just a little while. Well, I *do*.'

'Eli—'

'Yeah, you were right about me,' he continued, his mouth twisting in a bitter parody of a smile as she stared up at him. 'I was out on these streets for a year, so I know *exactly* what's it like.'

His face was harsh and white in the lamplight, and she didn't know what to do, what to say, so she did the only thing she could think of. She put her hand on his arm in what she hoped was a comforting gesture and, for a second, she thought it might have helped. For a second, she thought he was actually going to cover her fingers with his own, then he pulled his arm free with a muttered oath.

'Eli, don't give up hope,' she insisted, thinking he was going to walk away from her. 'Every time we go out we can keep an eye out for him, and maybe we'll get lucky, maybe we'll find him.'

He could see sympathy and pity in her eyes and something inside him broke. He didn't want her sympathy, or her pity. He didn't want to feel the urge to put his arms around her, and the desire to have her hold him back. He was Elijah Munroe, who had never in his life needed anyone, and he wasn't about to start now. Somehow she was managing to get past his defences, and he had to stop it, end it, and he lashed out at her with the only weapon he had left.

'What—no questions about my time on the streets?' he

jeered. 'Aren't you just longing for me to tell you all the gory, grisly details?'

She flinched, almost as though he had hit her, and he saw her eyes cloud with hurt.

'I thought…' He saw her shake her head. 'I hoped you might know me better than that. I would never intrude on something that's very personal to you.'

'Oh, of course, I forgot.' He nodded. 'Saint Brontë. Always the sympathetic, always the understanding. Little Miss Perfect.'

What little colour she had drained from her face.

'I'm not perfect—not by a long shot,' she said, and he could hear the tremble in her voice. 'I screw up just like everyone else, make mistakes as we all do—'

'You wanted to know whether I had any brothers or sisters?' he interrupted, hating to see the pain and bewilderment in her face, but it was preferable to sympathy and pity. 'I could have twelve for all I know because my mother dumped me in an orphanage when I was four. "I'll be gone for five minutes," she said, and then she disappeared, and I never saw her again.'

He waited for her to dish out the sympathy he knew he couldn't bear, because then he would be able to lash out at her again, but she didn't give him sympathy.

Instead, she said, 'Do you know why she left you?'

'Got fed up with me, I suppose,' he replied dismissively. 'Got fed up with having a whining brat hanging about her skirt all day, spoiling her life, and by all accounts I wasn't a very loveable child.'

Brontë didn't know whether he had been or not. All she knew was there was a world of hurt inside this man, a world of pain and self-hatred, and, though what he had said to her had been cruel, she had to swallow hard to subdue the tears she could feel clogging her throat.

'And your father?' she said hesitantly.

'I don't remember any man in the house, so I'm guessing I was a bastard.' He smiled. A tight smile that made her wince. 'Which is what you always believed I was, so you were right yet again, Miss O'Brian. Someone give the lady a prize.'

'How did you end up on the street?' she asked, longing to put her arms around him, to comfort him, but his rigid face told her that would be a very big mistake.

'I got fostered out a few times from the orphanage, but each family sent me back.' He shrugged. 'Too much trouble. Always getting into fights, always running away.'

'Because you were unhappy,' she protested. 'And what person—be they adult or child—wouldn't lose their temper, and keep running away, if they were suddenly uprooted from what they'd known all their lives and continually placed some-where alien, strange?'

'Yeah, well, by the time I was fourteen I'd had enough of being passed around as the parcel nobody wanted, so I ran away. I lived for a year on the streets in Edinburgh until one of the priests from a night shelter found me sleeping beside their dustbins. At first I thought he was pervert, after my youthful body,' Eli continued with an ironic laugh, 'and the poor bloke ended up with a black eye, and a broken nose.'

Brontë didn't laugh—she couldn't—and she knew he wasn't laughing either, not inside. She could picture him oh-so clearly in her mind; how frightened he must have been, how desperate.

'He took you in?' she said, trying to keep her voice as even as possible, but knowing she wasn't succeeding.

Eli nodded. 'He taught me how to read and write, gave me books, paper and pens, and then he started taking me out on his pastoral visits, and I met all these people. People who were ill. People who were dying.'

'And that's when you decided you wanted to become a nurse.'

'Yes.'

She stared down the dark and empty street for a few seconds, then back at him.

'Eli, there are ways of tracking down your mother. Societies who specialise in finding missing people. You could—'

'And why the hell should I want to find her?' he interrupted, his face dark and angry. 'She didn't want me. If she'd wanted me she would never have dumped me.'

'Maybe she had a good reason,' she said uncertainly. 'Maybe she didn't want to give you up, but she didn't have enough money to take care of you, or maybe she was very ill, and knew she couldn't cope.'

His lip curled.

'Saint Brontë, always the understanding, always the forgiving. Doesn't it ever get tiring living up on that damned pedestal of yours? No wonder men walk all over you, use you like a doormat, because that's exactly what you are!'

She stared up at him, her face ashen in the moonlight, and, as a clock tolled the hour in the distance, he saw her swallow, then hesitantly pull the ambulance ignition keys from her pocket and hold them out to him.

'It's half past six,' she said. 'Our shift's over so, I think... As I live just round the corner... Would you mind very much driving the ambulance back to the station for me?'

'Not a problem,' he said dismissively, and she backed up a step.

'It's just...I think...I would like to go home now,' she said.

'You do that,' he replied.

But, as he watched her trudge away through the snow, her shoulders hunched against the biting wind, he had to clench his hands together to stop himself from running after her. To stop himself from getting down on his knees and begging her to forgive him for the awful, unforgivable things he'd said.

It's better this way, he told himself when she turned the corner and he couldn't see her any more. Much better, he insisted, closing his eyes tightly against the snow which was beginning to fall again, and if he didn't feel that way at the moment he eventually would. Time, as he had discovered, could make you accept almost anything.

CHAPTER FIVE

Friday, 10:14 p.m.

'OKAY, I want to know what happened, and I want it in words of one syllable,' George Leslie declared, his normally amenable face tight and angry.

'I'd be more than happy to give you an answer if I knew what you were talking about.' Eli smiled as he rubbed down the windscreen of his ambulance, then tossed the chamois leather into the glove compartment.

'Ms O'Brian.'

Eli's smile disappeared in an instant. 'What about her?'

'Don't play the innocent with me,' his boss retorted. 'Three more shifts—that's all you had to keep a lid on your blasted temper for. Three shifts to be pleasant, and civil, but, no, you had to go and screw it up.'

'She's been complaining about me, has she?' Eli observed, his face an unreadable mask, and George Leslie grimaced reluctantly.

'She phoned me this afternoon to ask if she could be assigned to another ambulance because she felt she had upset you. Complete nonsense, of course,' George continued with a pointed glare at Eli. 'I know perfectly well if there was any upsetting going on you were at the root of it.'

'She thinks she's upset me?' Eli said incredulously, and his boss nodded.

'Frankly, I didn't believe a word of it either, but—'

'Who are you teaming her with?' Eli interrupted, and George Leslie threw his hands up with irritation.

'As I told Ms O'Brian, I can't team her with anyone else unless I do some massive alterations of people's shifts which will go down like a lead balloon with the other paramedics, and for three shifts it's just not worth the hassle, so she's stuck with you.'

'I see.'

'I don't think you do,' George Leslie observed. 'Eli, I want whatever has caused this friction sorted. She seems a pleasant enough person, not at all like a normal number cruncher—'

'She isn't.'

'—so can you *please* try not to rub her up the wrong way?'

'George—' Eli began, only to clamp his mouth shut.

The bay door had opened, and Brontë had stepped hesitantly onto the forecourt. George had seen her, too, and his eyebrows snapped down.

'I don't want to have this conversation with you again, Eli,' he declared in a hissed undertone. 'Understand?'

Eli didn't as his boss walked away. He didn't understand why Brontë hadn't simply told George he was impossible to work with. He fervently wished she had as he watched her square her shoulders as though preparing for his next onslaught. He had said such terrible things to her at the end of their last shift, things which still made him feel guilty, and he didn't want to feel guilty. He wanted his easy, uncomplicated, carefree life back again, not the woman who was so unsettling it.

'Cold night again,' Brontë declared hesitantly as she drew level with him. 'Minus twelve, according to the forecast, and there must be about six inches of snow on the roads now.'

'Yes,' he replied.

Heavens, but she looked so tired. He could see dark shadows under her eyes as though she hadn't slept well. He had slept badly, too, tossing and turning, unable to forget the look on her face before she'd turned and walked away from him.

'Hopefully we won't be as busy as we were last night,' she observed.

'Hopefully not.'

'Eli—'

'Brontë—'

They'd spoken in unison and, though he knew it was wrong, he took the coward's way out.

'You first,' he said, and saw her bite her lip, then take a deep breath.

'I saw you talking to George,' she said. 'I did try to get him to change the roster—to assign me to someone else—honestly I did, but he said it would be too difficult. I'm sorry.'

She looked it, too, he thought with mounting irritation. She looked as though she wanted to be anywhere but here, talking to anyone but him, and his guilt morphed into a much more convenient anger.

'Why the hell didn't you just tell George the truth?' he demanded. 'That I was rude and obnoxious to you last night, and you can't stand working with me?'

She looked confused.

'But that wouldn't have been the truth,' she said. 'I overstepped the mark—intruded into your private life—and you had every right to chew me out.'

He stared at her in disbelief. Surely she couldn't truly believe that? She must be being sarcastic, but there was nothing in her grey eyes except genuine regret, and he swore in exasperation.

'Dammit, Brontë. Must you always be so understanding, so accommodating, so…so damn *nice*? After what I said to you this morning… You should be calling me a low-life scumbag, and slapping my face!'

To his surprise, a hint of a smile appeared on her lips.

'I didn't know you were into S and M, as well as serial dating.'

'S and M…?' His mouth opened and closed soundlessly for a second, then he gazed heavenwards with frustration. 'Brontë, you are *impossible*.'

'Probably.' She nodded. 'You know, I'm really clocking up the labels since I started working with you. I always knew I was boring and ordinary—'

'You are not!'

'And now you've added middle-child syndrome, low self-esteem, doormat and impossible to my labels.'

'The doormat crack,' he said uncomfortably. 'That was totally out of order.'

'It would have been if I don't have a horrible suspicion you're right,' she replied ruefully. 'So, in a way, you did me a favour, and this morning I made a pledge. No more nice-girl Brontë. It's kick-ass Brontë from now on.'

'I'm glad to hear it,' he said, meaning it, 'but that doesn't absolve me from guilt. I was the jerk last night. Me, not you. *Me*.'

'But—'

'I was angry,' he interrupted. 'I know that's no excuse, but I was angry with Duncan for being so stupid. Angry with society for turning its back on youngsters like John, and…' He met her gaze. 'I was angry with you for somehow getting me to talk about myself, my past. I don't do that, you see. Not ever.'

'Maybe you should,' she said gently, her large grey eyes soft.

'The past is past,' he replied dismissively. 'It does no good to resurrect it, dwell on it, because nothing can be changed, altered.'

'No,' she agreed. 'But sometimes the past needs to be

faced, to be come to terms with, so it can't hurt you any more, and you can move on.'

'Like you getting over your lousy track record with men, and conquering your low self-esteem?' he suggested with a glimmer of a smile, and she smiled back.

'Exactly,' she said, then she tilted her head speculatively to one side, and he saw a glint of laughter appear in her eyes.

'What?' he asked warily.

'I'm just wondering whether you still wanted me to slap you?'

'Depends on how big a punch you pack,' he replied.

She laughed, and he tried to laugh, too, but all he could wonder was, How had she done that? One minute he had been so angry with her, and then the next... And he wanted to stay angry with her, because being angry was safe. Being angry meant she couldn't affect him, and being angry with her was infinitely preferable to the undeniable relief he had felt when he'd seen her smile.

Responsible, protective, his mind whispered, and he tried to crush down the nagging little voice, tried to make it go away, but it wouldn't go away, and when he heard the bleep of their MDT he beat Brontë into the ambulance by a long country mile.

'What have we got?' she asked as she joined him.

'LOL, 22 Jeffrey Street, Violet Young,' he replied. 'Neighbour can see her lying in the hallway, apparently unconscious, but can't get in because the front door is locked.'

'Well, I don't think that's even remotely funny,' Brontë muttered as she drove out of the bay.

'Sorry?' Eli replied in confusion, then the penny dropped and he laughed, properly this time. 'LOL doesn't mean "laughing out loud," as it does in chatspeak, Brontë. It means "little old lady."'

'Then why didn't the display say that?' she protested, and he smiled.

'Yeah, and like A and E doesn't have a language all of its own?'

He was right, it did, Brontë thought, trying not to smile back too fulsomely, but it didn't work, and she groaned inwardly.

What had happened to the pledge she'd made so sincerely this morning? The pledge the new kick-ass Brontë had made to be pleasant and yet detached, friendly and yet slightly aloof. All that resolve had disappeared in an instant under the spell of a pair of deep blue eyes and a killer smile.

Distance, she told herself. What she desperately needed was to maintain some distance, but how did you distance yourself from a man when your wayward heart kept letting you down? When you discovered the more you found out about him, the more you wanted to hold him, not because he was handsome, not because he could be so charming, but because of the pain and hurt you now knew he kept so carefully hidden from the world. She was a lost cause, and she knew it, but of one thing she was certain. He was never going to find out how she felt. Not ever.

'Lot of houses,' she said, deliberately changing the subject as she turned into Jeffrey Street, and saw the row of buildings stretching far ahead of her. 'Let's hope the numbers run concurrently.'

They did but, even if they hadn't, the neighbour who had called 999 was out on the snow-covered pavement and waved them down.

'I'm so glad you're here,' she declared the instant Eli and Brontë got out of the ambulance. 'Mrs Young… I thought she was just staying indoors today because of the snow, but her daughter phoned me half an hour ago. Said she couldn't get a reply when she dialled her mother's number, so I went round and…'

'She didn't answer when you rang the doorbell?' Eli said, and the neighbour shook her head.

'I looked through the letter box, and she's just lying there, in the hall, and…she's not moving.'

That the neighbour was deeply upset was clear, and Eli smiled at her encouragingly.

'Why don't you go back indoors now?' he suggested. 'We'll take it from here.'

The woman looked from Eli to Brontë, then back again. 'Are you sure? I don't want to leave my kids alone for too long, even though they're in bed, but if I can help…?'

'You've done more than enough already,' Eli insisted, and relief appeared instantly on the woman's face.

It was a relief Brontë would have felt herself if she'd been in the woman's shoes. There was just something about Eli that inspired confidence. Something which suggested if anyone could make things right he could. He was such an enigma, such a conundrum. Consummate professional, Good Samaritan and serial womaniser. Which of them was 'the real' Elijah Munroe? Maybe they all were. She wished she knew.

No, you don't, her head reminded her. *You're going to keep your distance, remember?* But, as she watched Eli crouch down to look through Mrs Young's letter box, she knew her pledge was a forlorn one.

'Can you see her?' she asked, and he nodded.

'She's at the very end of the hallway, and from the odd way she's lying, I'm thinking possible broken arm or leg, though it could be a CVA. The hall light's on which would suggest she collapsed—or fell—sometime this evening rather than earlier in the day.'

'Which is good news, isn't it?' Brontë replied, but Eli wasn't listening to her. He was running his hands over the door frame, and she stared at him incredulously. 'You're not thinking of trying to break down that door, are you?'

'Somewhat horrifyingly, you don't have to be superman to do it,' he murmured. 'That's just a normal front door key lock, and if you get the pressure dead centre, they break pretty easily.'

'They do?' Brontë gulped, thinking of the exact same lock she had on the front door of her own flat.

'A deadlock is much better any day of the week,' he observed, 'and if you add a bolt to the deadlock, you're even safer. To be completely secure you could put a bar across your front door, though that would mean if you collapsed behind it we wouldn't be able to get in to resuscitate you, but I guess you'd be a safe corpse.'

'Right,' Brontë replied, making a mental note to phone a joiner the minute she finished this shift.

That mental note became a certainty when she saw Eli stand back, take a deep breath, then hit the door squarely with his foot and the lock gave way instantly.

'I'm impressed,' she declared, then shook her head. 'No, I'm not. I'm horrified you can do that so easily.'

'It helps if you take a size eleven.' He grinned, then swore when, out of nowhere, an Alsatian dog suddenly appeared at the end of the hallway, its teeth bared in a deep growl. 'Oh, wonderful. Why didn't the neighbour tell us she had a dog?'

'What do we do now?' Brontë whispered, only to wonder why she was whispering because it wasn't as though the dog would understand what she was saying.

'We'll need to phone the cops. Get them to send out one of their dog handlers.'

'But Mrs Young…' Brontë protested. 'The longer we wait…'

'I know, but do you really want to take on Fang there?' Eli demanded, and Brontë stared at the dog.

She'd grown up with dogs. There had always been at least two at home when she, and Byron and Rossetti, had been growing up, and, though none of them had been quite as big as the Alsatian standing in the hallway, the dog's eyes looked more frightened than angry.

'Good dog,' she said softly, taking a step into the house. '*Nice* dog.'

'Are you *crazy*?' Eli hissed, catching hold of her arm, and the dog's growl became a snarl.

'I know what I'm doing,' Brontë said out of the corner of her mouth. Or, at least she hoped she did as she saw the dog crouch, and the hackles on its back rise. 'Let go of me, Eli.'

'But, Brontë…'

'*Lovely* doggy, we're not going to hurt you, or your mistress,' she continued, keeping her eyes fixed on the dog as she advanced another step. 'I know you're frightened, and we're strangers in your home, but we're here to help.'

The dog sat down. Its lip was still curled back over its teeth, and it hadn't taken its eyes off her for a second, but at least it no longer looked to be in 'I'm going to spring and rip out your throat' mode, and the snarling had lessened to a low, warning growl.

Faintly she could hear Eli muttering, and guessed he was telephoning the police to ask them to send out a dog handler. Or for someone to sweep up her remains, she thought wryly as she walked forward another step, watching the dog the whole time.

'*Nice* dog, *friendly* dog,' she crooned. 'Everything's going to be fine, just fine.'

She risked a quick glance at Mrs Young. She thought the elderly lady's chest was rising and falling slowly, and for a second she thought she saw her eyes flicker open, but she couldn't be sure. She could also see a dark blue plastic toy shaped like a bone, and an idea came into her head. It wasn't much of an idea, but it was better than nothing, and nothing was what she had at the moment.

Slowly, she bent down, and picked up the toy.

'Want to play fetch?' she asked.

The dog's tail thumped once against the floor, then stopped. It was clearly torn between a favourite game, and guarding its mistress, but the door to the sitting room was open, and if she could just lure the dog in that direction…

'Brontë…'

'Shut up, Eli,' she said, hoping her tone sounded more like an endearment than an order to the watching dog. 'Want to play fetch?' she repeated, waving the toy bone backwards and forwards slowly and saw the dog's head follow her movements.

It was now or never, she realised, and, taking a deep breath, she shouted, *'Fetch,'* then threw the toy as hard as she could into the sitting room. The Alsatian was off like a flash, following it, but Brontë was faster. The minute the dog was in the sitting room, she pulled the door shut, then leant against it, breathing hard, keeping her fingers tight round the handle.

'Was that the police you were phoning?' she asked as Eli brushed past her towards Mrs Young.

'They'll be here in three minutes,' he answered.

His voice was tight, cold, but she ignored that.

'I hope they make it faster,' she said instead, as a cacophony of growls, and scraping paws, began to fill the air, and the sitting room door juddered beneath her fingers. 'My parents used to have a dog who could turn any door handle with its teeth.'

Eli didn't reply. He was already setting up their heart monitor, and, though she wanted to go and help, the thought of one very angry dog suddenly bursting out of the sitting room was not an appealing one.

'How is Mrs Young?' she asked.

'Heart rate not too bad given her age, pulse a little weak, and my guess is her right leg is broken,' he answered.

And Eli clearly needed help, not her standing with her fingers clamped tightly round the sitting room door handle, so it was with a huge sigh of relief that Brontë greeted the burly, uniformed figure who suddenly appeared at the front door.

'I hear you have a dog problem?' The man grinned.

'You could say that,' Brontë admitted as the sound of barking and snarling intensified from inside the sitting room. 'Could you hold on to this door for me, and not open it until my colleague and I have taken the dog's owner to the Pentland?'

'No problem,' the dog handler replied, and, as soon as his hand had replaced hers on the door handle, Brontë hurried to Eli's side.

'What do you want me to do?'

'Get an Ambu bag on her, and then we go,' he declared. 'She's very, very cold, which means she's been lying here for quite some time.'

'She has a name, young man,' Mrs Young murmured faintly, and Eli smiled down at her.

'So, you're awake, are you, Mrs Young?'

'No, I just talk when I'm unconscious,' she muttered. 'Of course I'm awake. I just don't seem to be able to *stay* awake.'

Brontë's eyes met Eli's. Hypothermia. There was a very strong possibility that Mrs Young was suffering from hypothermia as well as a broken leg.

'I'm afraid we're going to have to take you to the hospital, Mrs Young,' she said gently and saw a flicker of alarm cross the old lady's face.

'But what about Bubbles? You'll have to phone my daughter, tell her to come and take care of him because I can't leave Bubbles on his own.'

The Alsatian who was currently trying to tear down the sitting room door was called *Bubbles*? Brontë glanced across at Eli to share the joke but, oddly enough, he didn't seem to find it nearly as amusing as she did.

'My colleague is just going to put this Ambu bag on you,

Mrs Young,' he declared, 'and then it's off to the hospital for you. And, yes, I'll get someone to phone your daughter about Bubbles,' he added as the old lady began to protest, 'so stop worrying about him and start thinking about yourself.'

A small smile appeared on Mrs Young's lips, and she transferred her gaze to Brontë.

'Is he always this bossy, dear?' she said, and Brontë nodded.

'I'm afraid so,' she relied. 'In fact, he's notorious for it so, if I were you, I'd just give in gracefully.'

Mrs Young did and, once the Ambu bag was in place, they lifted her into a carry-chair, and quickly out to the ambulance.

'I'd say she's going to be okay, wouldn't you?' Brontë said to Eli after they'd delivered Mrs Young into the waiting arms of the A and E staff. 'I know she's elderly, and if you break a leg at that stage in your life it can really knock you for six, but her heart rate was strong, and she seems a spunky, never-say-die lady.'

'I'd bet money on her being back home within the month,' Eli replied as they walked through the waiting room to the exit.

'Her daughter seemed nice, too,' Brontë continued. 'And I'm so pleased she's going to look after Bubbles. I know you didn't take to it,' she added, seeing Eli's jaw tighten, 'but it was only trying to protect its mistress.'

Eli said nothing.

'I know it looked a bit scary,' Brontë continued, 'but you have to look at it from its point of view. Its mistress wasn't moving, and we were strangers in its home.' Eli's silence was now positively deafening, and Brontë blew out a huff of impatience. 'Okay, you're clearly itching to chew my head off, so why don't you just do it, and get it over with?'

Eli waited until they were safely out on the street, and then he rounded on her.

'What you did—with that dog,' he said through clenched teeth, 'was either the bravest thing I've ever seen, or the stupidest.'

'And my guess is you're favouring the stupidest,' she said with a smile, but he didn't smile back.

'I said we should wait for the dog handler,' he declared, 'but did you listen to me, obey me? No, of course you didn't—'

'Eli, I know dogs—'

'You know every dog in the world?' he flared. 'Whoa, but that must make you pretty unique.'

'I didn't mean I know every dog,' she protested, 'but I weighed up the situation, took a calculated risk—'

'One which almost had me flat out on the floor beside Mrs Young with a heart attack!'

He wasn't joking. She could tell from his taut face, and angry eyes, he wasn't joking, and she bit her lip.

'Look, I'm sorry if you were worried, but I was watching the dog's eyes, and I thought it seemed more frightened than anything else.'

'You thought—you *thought*!' He muttered something unprintable under his breath. 'Brontë, you had no way of knowing what that dog might do. It could have bitten you very badly, torn your hand off—'

'But it didn't,' she insisted. 'I'm not a fool—'

'Do you really want me to comment on that?'

'—and if it had looked completely out of control I would have waited for the dog handler. I *would*,' she insisted as he shook his head at her, 'but with dogs it's generally their eyes you go by. Their eyes, and their body language.'

'And that's the biggest load of rubbish I've ever heard,' he retorted. '*All* dogs are unpredictable. *All* dogs can turn into killing machines, and the bigger they are, the more damage they can inflict. I remember once, when I was living on the streets…' He closed his eyes, then opened them again. 'Let's just say I don't even want to think about what happened to the poor bloke, far less talk about it.'

She stared silently at him for a second, and when she spoke her voice was low, contrite. 'I'm sorry…I didn't realise…. Were you really that worried about me?'

It took him all his self-control not to reach out, grab her by the shoulders and shake her. Worried? His heart had practically stopped when she'd walked towards that dog, looking so small, so vulnerable, but he didn't say that.

'If you put your hand on my chest you'll feel my heart still going like a train,' he said instead.

A tinge of colour appeared on her cheeks, and she laughed a little shakily.

'I'll take your word for it,' she said, then cleared her throat. 'I really am sorry. I promise I won't ever do something like that again.'

'Is that a solemn "cross your heart and hope to die" promise?' he demanded, and when she hesitated, as though having to consider his question, his eyebrows snapped together. *'Brontë!'*

'Just kidding,' she said with a smile. 'It's a promise.'

He fervently hoped it was as they went back to their ambulance. He didn't ever want to go through another ten minutes like that ever again.

Protective, responsible, the irritating little voice in his head whispered again, and he tried to shut it up, to tell the annoying voice he would have felt the same concern for anyone, but the little voice simply laughed and, as it did, the answer suddenly came to him. An answer that was so blindingly obvious in its simplicity he wondered why he hadn't thought of it before.

Why in the world was he angsting like this? he wondered as Brontë drove away from the hospital. He was attracted to her, and he was pretty sure she was attracted to him, so all he needed to do was ask her out. His no-dating pledge only had three weeks left to run anyway, so what did it matter if he cut it short? He would simply ask her out, they'd go out on a few dates, become lovers and then, once he'd got her out of his system, he'd move on as he always did, with the problem solved, the angsting over.

'What's funny?'

'Funny?' he repeated, glancing across at Brontë in confusion.

'You're smiling,' she observed, 'so I just thought… If you've got a good joke I could sure do with hearing it.'

The joke was on him, he thought, because the solution had been there all the time, staring him right in the face, and yet for some unaccountable reason he hadn't been able to see it. He could see it now. He was back on familiar territory now, and it felt good.

'Brontë, I was wondering,' he began, only to groan when their MDT bleeped into life.

'"Code amber. RTC. Male aged thirty-two,"' Brontë read. '"Junction of College Street and Nicolson Street. Two cars involved. One casualty with whiplash. Other driver uninjured. Police in attendance."' She frowned. 'Sounds like a possible shunt to me, if only one person is hurt.'

'My guess is it's a payment point,' Eli replied, wishing the casualty to the farthest side of the moon as Brontë turned onto the North Bridge.

'A what?' she asked.

'In RTCs almost half of those supposedly suffering from whiplash are actually people who are attempting to get the insurance money out of the other driver,' Eli explained. 'And the "payment point" is the part of the neck they keep pointing to, and declaring they're in agony.'

'We didn't call them "payment points" in A and E at the Waverley,' Brontë declared. 'We called them PITAs.'

'And I don't need my nursing diploma to guess what that acronym stands for.' Eli laughed. 'And it just about sums these jokers up. They waste our time, the police's time, and put the other driver through hell, and all for money.'

'Isn't that why RTAs are now called RTCs?' Brontë observed as she headed for Nicolson Street. 'Because some smart lawyers figured out if the police described a car crash as an accident, their clients would be off the hook?'

'Yup.' Eli nodded. 'So now we have road traffic collisions, but we still get the payment-point brigade.'

The policeman who was waiting beside the two cars when they arrived clearly thought Eli's diagnosis was the correct one.

'He's kicking up a real racket—swears he's in total agony,' he declared, 'but the idiot keeps forgetting which part of his neck is supposed to be hurt. It's the poor woman in the other car I feel sorry for. Her car got the worst of it, and she can't stop shaking.'

She couldn't, and it took Brontë a good fifteen minutes to calm the woman down, and persuade her there was nothing she could do here, and she really should phone for a taxi and go home.

'How's our whiplash patient?' she asked when she was eventually able to join Eli by the other car.

Eli rolled his eyes heavenwards. 'What do you think?'

'The Pentland?' she said, and he nodded.

'I know it goes against the grain to transport someone we believe is faking it to hospital,' he replied, 'but there's always the possibility—no matter how remote—that an X-ray will reveal an injury I've missed.'

Eli was right, but Brontë couldn't help but think, as she drove towards the hospital, that it was hard to feel sympathetic towards a 'casualty' who, despite constantly protesting he was in the most appalling pain, still managed to make a dozen phone calls on his mobile phone.

That journey—and their patient—pretty well set the tone for the next few hours. The sensible Edinburgh citizens might have decided after last night's road chaos to stay home and keep safe, but there were still enough of the young, and the just plain cavalier, out on the streets, to keep Eli and Brontë busy until well after four o'clock.

'And it's snowing again,' Brontë said irritably as she drove down the Canongate, and had to switch on her windscreen wipers to clean her screen. 'Which no doubt means even more idiots will decide it might be a "fun" idea to take to the roads, and see how far they get before they skid and hit something.'

'Or someone.'

She knew who he was thinking of, and she glanced across at him quickly.

'I've been looking for him, Eli,' she said. 'When I've been driving along… Every time I pass a group of kids, or some homeless people, I've been looking for John.'

'Me, too,' Eli replied. 'It's been so cold these past couple of nights, Brontë, so very, very cold. I keep hoping he's got a room in one of the shelters, but there's so little accommodation available.'

'Do you think Peg will be all right?' she asked tentatively, and saw him force a smile.

'Peg's a pretty tough cookie. If anyone can survive, she can, but there are so many homeless people out there. When I see elderly people like Mrs Young, I think of the long lives they've had, the happy memories they must be able to look back on, but young addicts, young alcoholics…' Eli shook his head. 'All I can think is, How did you get lost, how did you lose your way? Other kids your age will have a life, a family, friends, but you… Your life is going to be so short. So very, very short.'

'My brother, Byron, has this theory,' she observed. 'He says people make their own choices in life.'

'That's true to a certain extent,' Eli replied, 'but what power did we—as a society—give these young people to enable them to make any kind of choice?'

'Eli—'

'Sorry—sorry,' he interrupted with a rueful smile. 'It's one of my pet hobby horses, and I shouldn't inflict it on you.'

'You're not inflict—'

'Coffee. I need a coffee,' he insisted, 'so let's head for Tony's.'

He saw her hesitate, then take a deep breath.

'Actually, I've been thinking about what you said before—about me not having met or spoken to any of the other paramedics at the station,' she said in a rush. 'You made a very good point, so I think we should take our break at the station tonight.'

Damn, but that was the last thing he needed, to be surrounded by his colleagues, when what he wanted was some privacy so he could ask her out.

'Good idea, in principle,' he observed lightly, 'but Friday nights… They're always busy, everyone flat out, so there's little likelihood there will be anybody for you to talk to.'

'Oh.'

She didn't look happy, but he wasn't about to waver, and so he smiled what he hoped was his best encouraging smile.

'Tony's?' he said, and thought he heard her sigh with resignation as she nodded, but he couldn't be sure.

Brontë was sure. Brontë didn't want to go anywhere near Tony's tonight. She wanted to be safe amongst a crowd. She wanted other people to distract her, not to be sitting alone in an ambulance with Eli, but she would rather have stuck a fork in her eye than admit that to him.

Be pleasant, and yet detached, she reminded herself when she pulled up outside Tony's. That's all you have to be. Pleasant, detached, and slightly aloof. How hard could that be?

Damned hard, she thought as he got out of the ambulance,

then turned to look at her with the smile which always made all rational conversation disappear instantly from her brain.

'Cappuccino and doughnut?' he said.

She thought about it. 'A cappuccino, for sure, but tonight I want a hamburger. A big, juicy hamburger, with lots of onions.'

His eyebrows rose, but he didn't say anything until he returned to the ambulance with their orders.

'Never thought I'd see you eat one of those,' he observed, as she bit into the hamburger, then closed her eyes, clearly relishing the taste.

'Yeah, well, you're corrupting me.'

'Am I?'

It could have been a completely innocuous observation. It could have been the kind of joking thing a friend would have said, but it wasn't, and she knew it wasn't. His voice was suddenly low, velvety, within the silence of the ambulance, and the atmosphere had changed—she could feel it, sense it, but this time she knew what he was doing; this time she was prepared, and she opened her eyes, and met his gaze full on.

'Only for hamburgers,' she said.

'Really?'

His voice was teasing, liquid, and she felt her heart pick up speed.

'Really,' she replied firmly, wishing he would just let it go, would stop, but he didn't.

Instead, he looked at her over the rim of his coffee, his eyes dark and oh-so blue. 'Care to make a wager on that?'

She took another mouthful of hamburger, and swallowed it with difficulty, all too aware her heart rate had now gone into overdrive.

'Nope,' she replied. 'Not interested, not a betting woman.'

'Then maybe I can offer you something you *will* be interested in,' he said softly.

This wasn't merely flirting, she realised as her eyes met his, and what she saw there made her stomach lurch and her pulses race. This was something more, and, though part of her wanted to tell him to stop, to say nothing else, the other part—the weak, traitorous part—wanted to hear what he was going to say, and it was that part which won.

'I'm listening,' she said.

He put down his coffee.

'Brontë, I know you think I'm smug, and arrogant—'

'And a bit of a prat at times,' she interrupted. 'Don't forget the "bit of a prat."'

'It's engraved on my heart,' he said lightly, though she could see she had rattled him. 'But the thing is… You're a very special woman, Brontë.'

He was going to ask her out. He was going to ask her out, and, though she knew exactly what she should say in reply, knowing it didn't mean she was necessarily going to do it.

'Go on,' she said, taking a slow sip of her coffee more to buy herself some time than from any real thirst.

'Without being vain,' he continued, 'I think you like me, too, so I was wondering whether you'd like to come out to dinner with me before our shift tomorrow?'

She stared down at her coffee, then up at him.

'To dinner?' she repeated slowly. 'Now, are we just talking dinner here, or are we talking something more?'

He smiled his killer smile.

'Oh, come on, Brontë, we're both adults, and I think you and I could really have some fun together.'

Some fun together. Not a proper relationship, not the possibility of that relationship ever leading to something more permanent, but just some 'fun', and her heart constricted with pain and disappointment as she stared at his handsome face. Pain and disappointment which were very quickly overtaken by anger. A blazing furious anger with herself for yet again being so naive to hope he might have offered more, and an equally furious anger with him for believing she had so little self-worth she would even consider settling for what he usually offered the women in his life.

Carefully, she put her coffee down on the dashboard in case she was tempted to do something rash with it.

'And how long would this "fun" last?' she asked, keeping her voice neutral with difficulty.

He blinked. 'Sorry?'

'I'm just wondering, you see,' she observed, 'whether I'd get the usual two months with you, or whether I might get real lucky and be allowed a little bit longer.'

His dark eyebrows snapped together.

'I don't think that comment was necessary,' he replied icily, and she forced herself to shrug.

'I would have said I was just being realistic,' she replied, 'because, you see, what you call "fun," results in a hell of a lot of heartbreak for a lot of women, so it's a road I'm rather reluctant to travel down.'

'I have never in my whole life broken any woman's heart!' he exclaimed. 'I've always been upfront, never promised I'd stick around for ever.'

Why could he not see it? she wondered. Why did he keep on denying what was so obvious to her?

'Eli, are you blind, or stupid, or both?' she demanded. 'Can't you see—don't you understand—that it doesn't matter how upfront you think you're being? I doubt if there's a woman alive who, when you've asked her out, hasn't thought, This is for keeps, this is going to last. No matter what you say, no matter how hard you try to persuade them you're only dating them for "fun," they think, Me. He's going to settle down with me because I can change him.'

'I don't believe that,' he retorted, and she shook her head at him.

'That's because, for all your talk, you know *nothing* about women. You just take and take, and give nothing of yourself. Dating—sex—it's all a no-risk game to you, isn't it? Don't let anyone close, don't let anyone into your mind, and heart.'

'And you're such an expert on dating, are you?' he snapped, and hot, furious colour stained her cheeks.

'At least I *tried*!' she exclaimed. 'At least when I went into a relationship, I went into it wholeheartedly not thinking I'll just have some "fun," then dump the guy. Okay, so maybe my relationships didn't work out, and I ended up getting my face pushed in the mud, and my heart trampled in the dirt—'

'A bit difficult to have those two things done to you at once,' he interrupted sarcastically, and she moved beyond anger into incensed.

'Must you make a joke out of *everything*?'

'Look, listen—'

'No, *you* listen,' she broke in, her grey eyes blazing. 'Relationships, love—everything's one big game to you, and do you want to know why? It's because—deep down—you're a coward. You play at everything, never letting anyone get close to the real you, hiding behind this…this supercool image when, in reality, you're just a coward. I know your mother hurt you very badly—'

'Leave my mother out of this.'

His voice was low, dangerous, but she'd started and she couldn't stop.

'And maybe her leaving you resulted in you having trust issues—'

'You're saying I've set out to make every woman pay for what my mother did?' he exclaimed in disbelief, and she exhaled with exasperation.

'Of course I'm not saying that,' she replied. 'What I'm saying is I think you're scared to get too close to anyone in case you get hurt again.'

He shook his head impatiently.

'That is the biggest load of psychobabble I've ever heard.'

'It makes just as much sense as you telling me I have lousy taste in men because I have middle-child syndrome,' she countered, and he crushed the paper bag which contained his uneaten hamburger between his fingers.

'I've had enough of this conversation.'

'You were the one who started it,' she pointed out, and he rounded on her.

'Then I'm the one who's finishing it!'

'Fine.' She nodded. 'Throw a hissy fit, sit there in a snit, because you don't like the truth when you hear it, but you can do it on your own.'

'Where the hell are you going?' he demanded as she opened the driver's door, and got out.

'Back to the station where the air is less toxic.'

'Don't be ridiculous,' he declared. 'You can't walk back through The Meadows at half past four in the morning. Heaven knows what weirdos you're likely to meet at this hour.'

'I'll take my chances.'

'You're being stupid.'

She knew she was as she slammed the door, and walked away. Crossing The Meadows on her own at half past four in the morning was not a smart idea. Crossing The Meadows when the snow was falling in ever-increasing, large, whirling flakes was even crazier. Even if no one approached her she would still have all those streets to walk unless she could find a taxi, but she had to get away from him. She had to get away because she knew if she didn't she was going to burst into tears, and no way was she going to give him the satisfaction of knowing she cared so much, and so stupidly longed to be the one woman who might change him.

'Brontë, wait a minute!'

She heard the sound of his door closing, then a muttered oath which meant he'd tripped over something. Serve him right, she decided grimly, not slowing her stride by an inch. If he thought shouting at her some more would get him any-where, he was dumber than a rock.

'Brontë.'

He had caught up with her, but, when he clasped her shoulder and tried to turn her to face him, she shrugged him off.

'Go away, Eli. Just…just go away!'

'But I want to talk to you,' he insisted, coming round in front of her, barring her way.

'Then you're going to be sadly disappointed,' she retorted, trying her hardest to sound indifferent, but unfortunately a wayward tear slid down her cheek.

'Oh, jeez, *don't*,' he said, staring at her in complete horror. 'Brontë, please, don't cry.'

'I'm not,' she replied, her voice betraying her. 'I just… I've simply got something in my eye.'

And desperately she wiped her nose with the back of her hand, and it was that small action which cut him to the bone. That completely uncalculated, almost childlike, defiant little action which stirred and touched something deep inside him, something he couldn't pinpoint or define.

'You're getting wet,' he said, reaching out and gently brushing the snowflakes from her hair and eyelashes. 'Please come back to the ambulance before you catch your death of cold.'

'Old wives' tale,' she replied, her voice thick. 'Germs cause colds, not getting wet.'

'Do you always have to have the last word?' he demanded, putting his hands on her shoulders in case she was thinking of walking away.

It was all he meant to do, just to keep her there, to stop her from doing anything rash, but, as he gazed down into her tear-filled eyes, she suddenly sniffed, and wiped her nose again, and those two actions were his undoing. Before he could think, before he could even rationalise what he was about to do, he bent his head and kissed her.

He meant it only to be a light kiss, a gentle kiss, but, as her lips opened under his, and he tasted her sweetness, her softness, and heard her give a small, shuddering sigh, that light kiss wasn't enough. Before he could stop himself, he had wrapped his arms around her, bringing her closer, closer, intensifying the kiss, deepening it, until all he was aware of was the fire and heat within him, and the need never to let her go.

And Brontë felt it, too, the same fire, the same heat, the same need, and she wound her arms round his neck, tasting him, his warmth, wanting so much to touch him, to feel his skin, but their bulky high-visibility jackets prevented that touch.

I want him, she thought, as she threaded her fingers through his hair to bring him closer, returning his kisses with a depth to match his own. I have always wanted him right from the first moment I saw him in Wendy's hallway when he walked right past me, but I can't let this continue because he'll leave me. He'll leave me just as he's left every other woman he's kissed, and it was that certainty which gave her the strength to jerk herself out of his arms, and back away from him.

'Don't, Eli, *don't*,' she said, her voice breaking on a sob. 'Don't flirt with me, play with me, lead me to believe you really care, because I can't stand it.'

'Brontë—'

'I'm not like you,' she said blindly. 'I can't live the way you do—being with one person one month, then another the next—and if I let myself get too close to you, you'll break my heart, and I don't think I'll ever be able to put the pieces back together again.'

'I would never break your heart,' he protested, his breathing harsh and erratic in the silence, and he reached for her again, only to see her back away still further.

'You might not mean to, you might not intend to, but you *will*.'

'Brontë—'

'Answer me one question,' she interrupted. 'How long would I get with you before you move on to someone else?'

He thrust his hands through his wet hair, his face impatient.

'How can I answer that?' he exclaimed. 'We'd just take it one day at a time, like every other couple do.'

'But we wouldn't be like every other couple, would we?' she cried. 'Because you've already told me you never want to settle down with just one woman, and I…' She took a long, juddering breath. 'I'm thirty-five years old, Eli, and I don't want what you call "fun." I want someone who will be there for me, someone who will care for me, someone…' Her voice broke again. 'Someone who will *love* me, and that's not you, is it?'

She saw indecision, and uncertainty, war with one another on his face, and then he shook his head.

'I'm sorry,' he murmured.

'So am I,' she said but, as she turned to go, he put his hand out to stop her.

'I won't let you walk back through The Meadows alone. If…' He bit his lip. 'If you can't bear to sit beside me in the ambulance I'll walk back to the station instead.'

'You could get mugged just as easily as me,' she pointed out, and he forced a smile.

'I'm bigger than you, tougher.'

'Are you?' she said, then shook her head. 'We'll go back together, but I want you to promise me something. I want you to promise there'll be no more flirting, or flattery, and definitely no more kisses, because I can't take any more of this. I really can't.'

He didn't say anything. He simply nodded and, as she walked back to the ambulance, not looking at him, not saying anything, all she could think was it didn't matter if he kept his promise because it was too late. She was already in love with him, and her heart was already breaking.

CHAPTER SIX

Sunday, 12:15 a.m.

SHE'D always hated Saturday nights at the Waverley, Brontë remembered as she drove over the North Bridge. Saturday nights in A and E meant drunks, and RTCs, chaos and mayhem. They meant exactly the same thing for the ambulance service. From the minute they'd clocked on she and Eli had been working flat out and for that, at least, Brontë was grateful. Working flat out meant they hardly had time to talk to each other. Working flat out meant no awkward silences, or uncomfortable pauses.

Oh, who was she kidding? she thought, as she risked a quick glance at Eli. She'd expected tonight to be difficult, but what she hadn't expected was for Eli to be so angry. Not an obvious anger, not a blatant anger, but a simmering, bubbling, undercurrent of anger she could feel, almost taste, and normally she would have moved into what her brother, Byron, called her 'make everyone happy' mode. She would have talked and talked until she was sick to death of the sound of her own voice, but tonight she didn't.

Tonight she was tired, and weary. Tired from tossing and turning sleeplessly, and weary from alternatively telling herself she'd made the right decision, and then berating herself for being an idiot not to have simply grabbed those two months from Eli and enjoyed them while she could.

'Left, you should have taken a left there for Bread Street,' Eli declared as she turned right at the junction.

'Are you sure?' she replied. 'I thought it would be faster if I cut along the Grassmarket?'

'It's not.'

'Right,' she muttered, and began to reverse back up the street.

'What on earth are you doing?' Eli exclaimed.

'Going back,' she protested. 'You said, turn left—'

'That doesn't mean I expected you to reverse back up a one-way street!'

Damn, but she hadn't even seen the one-way warning sign, and swiftly she drove back down the road, crunching the gears so badly even she winced.

'Sorry,' she mumbled.

'You do realise this detour means not only is our patient still waiting, we also can't possibly hit our target arrival time?'

'I *said* I was sorry,' she retorted. 'I made a mistake, okay, and I'm *sorry*.'

Just tonight and tomorrow night, she told herself as she drove on and heard Eli mutter something which didn't sound like, 'Apology accepted.' I've only got to get through tonight, and tomorrow night, and then I'll never have to see him again, but how was she going to get through those two shifts when she doubted if she could stand even another hour in his company?

'Watch the corners,' Eli declared as she took one too fast. 'There's at least a foot of snow out there now, and it's fallen on ice.'

'Look, would you prefer to drive instead of me?' she snapped.

'Perhaps I should, if you're going to be silly,' he replied

tersely, and she gripped the steering wheel until her knuckles showed white to stop herself from decking him.

Silly. He thought she was silly. Well, maybe she was, to have fallen in love with a man who quite patently didn't give a damn about her unless it was to add another notch to his bedpost. If anyone had the right to be angry, it was her. His heart wasn't broken. He would go on and find someone else fast enough, whereas she… She swallowed painfully as she cut across town, then came down Bread Street. Don't think, she told herself, don't remember the touch of his lips, his hands, because that's a fool's game.

'You've just gone straight past the house,' Eli declared. 'It's number 22, Bread Street.'

She knew it was. The caller had said, 'Harry Wallace, twenty-nine years old, in an apparently catatonic state, his mother with him, number 22, Bread Street,' and yet she'd gone right past the house without even noticing.

Pull yourself together, her mind whispered as she turned the ambulance too fast and swore as she felt the wheels spin slightly on the compacted snow. *This patient needs you, so pull yourself together.*

And Eli stared grimly out of the window, and was tempted to ask Brontë what her problem was, except he already knew the answer. According to her, he was the problem, and that accusation only made him all the angrier.

If she had simply turned down his dinner invitation this morning, he could have lived with it. Okay, he would have been irritated, annoyed, because women didn't normally turn down the chance to become involved with him, but she hadn't simply turned him down. She'd said she wouldn't go out with him because he had broken too many hearts which was nonsense. Okay, so Zoe had created the mother and father of all scenes when he'd left her, but that was because he'd made a mistake, not because he'd left a trail of heartbroken women in his wake.

'Will I take the defibrillator, just in case?' Brontë asked as she pulled the ambulance to a halt, and opened her door.

'You should know by now we always take everything,' he replied acidly.

She opened her mouth, then clamped her lips shut, and he had to bite down hard on the angry words that sprang to his lips, too, as she retrieved the defibrillator, then stomped up the path to the house. The sooner she was out of his life, the better. The sooner she left the station, the quicker he would forget her, and her troubling accusations.

And her kiss? his heart whispered. *Will you forget that, too?*

It was just a kiss, he told himself. No different from any other woman's kiss, but no matter how often he had told himself that since this morning he knew it wasn't true. It had been a kiss like no other kiss. A kiss that had made him feel as though he had somehow—oddly—finally come home, and he didn't want to feel like that, or even think it.

'I'm so glad you're here,' Mrs Wallace said when she answered Brontë's knock. 'My son…Harry…he suffers from bipolar depression. I don't know whether he's been deliberately not taking his medication, forgotten to take it, or if this is something new, but I came round when I couldn't get an answer to any of my phone calls, and…' She spread her arms helplessly. 'He's just sitting there.'

Harry Wallace was, and though both Eli and Brontë attempted to get some response from him, Harry either wouldn't, or couldn't, communicate.

'Is this the only medication your son is taking, Mrs Wallace?' Eli asked, lifting a bottle of pills from the mantelpiece, then putting it back down again.

'I'm afraid I don't know,' Harry's mother replied. 'He was diagnosed with bipolar almost ten years ago, and he's been on so many different pills since then. His bathroom cabinet's full of bottles, some with just a few pills in them, some completely full.'

'Show me,' Eli said and, as he followed Mrs Wallace out of the room, Brontë chewed her lip.

Discovering what pills Harry Wallace had in his bathroom wouldn't be hugely helpful. Knowing what he was currently taking, however, would, and, quickly, she crossed to the mantelpiece, and lifted the bottle of pills. As she'd hoped, they had a GP's name on them and she pulled her mobile phone out of her pocket.

That the GP was not happy about being called at one o'clock in the morning was plain, but he eventually gave her a list of Harry Wallace's current medications, and she had just finished writing the names down on a scrap of paper when Eli and Mrs Wallace returned to the sitting room.

Who are you talking to? Eli mouthed at her, and she turned the piece of paper over, scribbled the word GP on it, and held it up to him. To her complete bewilderment he began making slicing motions across his throat, clearly wanting her to end the call, but she had no intention of being so rude, not when she'd just asked the GP whether he could come to Bread Street.

'Brontë, *end the call.*'

She could hear the barely suppressed anger in Eli's voice, and she gritted her teeth. It was one thing to be angry with her over something personal, but when he brought that personal antagonism into their professional lives…

'Thanks for your help, Dr Simpson,' she said into her mobile phone, flipped it shut and turned to face Eli. 'Harry's GP is coming, and I have a list of the medications he should be taking.'

Eli took the piece of paper she was holding out to him, then smiled reassuringly at Mrs Wallace.

'As we're not sure whether Harry has simply missed a dose, perhaps inadvertently taken more than he should, or the medication is no longer controlling his bipolar, I think it would be best if we take him to hospital, and let the experts examine him.'

'But, Eli, Dr Simpson is on his way here,' Brontë declared pointedly, but she might just as well have been talking to the wall because he was already helping Harry Wallace to his feet.

'If you'd like to come with us, Mrs Wallace,' Eli said, 'you're more than welcome.'

But I'm clearly not, Brontë thought, as Mrs Wallace reached for her coat and Eli ushered Harry out into the hall without even a backward glance at her.

What in the world was he doing? Okay, so he was clearly still angry with her about what had happened in The Meadows last night, but Dr Simpson was going to arrive and find Harry Wallace's house in darkness. Well, it wasn't good enough, she decided, and she was going to tell Eli that in no uncertain terms after Harry had been safely admitted to the Pentland.

It took longer than she'd thought. Harry Wallace seemed to be quite well known to the staff of A and E, and to Men's Medical, and it was more than forty minutes before they could finally get away, but the waiting didn't decrease Brontë's anger. If anything, it fuelled it because Eli seemed to be simmering, too, and when she drove away from the hospital, she didn't drive far. Just round the corner, then she pulled the ambulance to a halt.

'Okay, I want an explanation, and it had better be a good one!' she exclaimed. 'It's one thing to be angry with me personally, but when it affects a patient's treatment—'

'Brontë—'

'You're obviously in a major strop because I got a list of the medications Harry Wallace is currently taking,' she interrupted, not even bothering to hide her fury. 'All right, so I thought of phoning his GP, and you didn't, but what the heck does that matter? I know you're the accredited paramedic, and I'm not, but surely a good idea is still a good idea?'

'Brontë—'

'And I persuaded Dr Simpson to come round to the house,' she continued, on a roll now. 'Dr Simpson, who, I might add, is going to have a completely wasted journey because you simply bundled Harry into the ambulance and took him to hospital!'

'How do you know Dr Simpson is coming?' Eli said with a calmness which was infuriating.

'Because he *told* me he would!' she retorted. 'Did you want to talk to him yourself—is that what this is all about? You're piqued because the number cruncher took the phone call?'

'I'll ignore that,' he replied, his tone considerably harder than hers, 'but I will repeat, what proof do you have Dr Simpson is on his way?'

She stared at him blankly. 'What are you talking about? I phoned him—'

'Brontë, we *never* call a GP from a landline, or a mobile. If we need to speak to a GP, or a social worker, or a CPN, we ask EMDC to call them for us because then all the telephone conversations are recorded, which means if someone says they are going to attend they'd better.'

'But—'

'There are some wonderful GPs out there, some terrific social workers,' Eli continued, 'but there's a small minority who are more than happy to shunt all their responsibility onto the ambulance services rather than getting off their butts and doing what they're paid for. With no way of proving your phone call, we could be sitting in that house until doomsday waiting for your Dr Simpson, and he could deny he'd ever made that promise.'

Eli was right, Brontë realised with dismay as she stared at him, but knowing it didn't make her feel any better.

'Why didn't you tell me this before?' she demanded. 'If you'd just told me, kept me in the loop—'

'How was I to know you were going to do something stupid?'

Stupid. He thought she was stupid. He thought she was stupid, and silly, and a doormat, and the hurt she had felt ever since he'd thrown that last epithet at her, combined with the pain she still felt from realising all he had wanted from her was 'fun' , brought tears to her throat. Tears she was never going to let him see.

'Okay. Fine,' she said with difficulty. 'You know every-thing, and I'm the village idiot, so in future I'll simply drive your ambulance, and the only words I'll speak will be, "Where to?"'

'And now you really *are* being stupid,' he threw back at her.

She didn't say a word. She simply started the engine, and drove off down the road, but she didn't get far before their MDT began flashing a message.

'Suspected purple in the Potterrow. Police officer in at-tendance. Young boy who doesn't appear to be breathing.'

Brontë's eyes shot to Eli's. A 'purple' was ambulance code-speak for someone who was dead, but that wasn't the word on the screen which had caused her to suck in her breath sharply. It was the word *boy*.

Please, don't let it be him, she prayed, as she shot off down the road, heedless of the icy, snowy conditions. Please let it be somebody else, anyone else. She knew Eli was thinking the same, could see it in the tense way he was sitting next to her. He had tried so hard to help John Smith, and if the young boy was him…

'I'm afraid there's nothing you can do here, folks,' the police officer said when she and Eli got out of the ambulance. 'Judging by how cold he is I'd say he's been dead for a couple of hours. No sign of foul play that I can see so my guess is hyperthermia, though on these streets it could well be drug-related even though he's just a kid.'

A kid who was wearing a pair of threadbare trainers, thin denim trousers, and a tattered wine-coloured jacket, Brontë realised as she walked slowly towards the small figure lying huddled in the shop doorway.

Why did it have to be him? she wondered as she knelt down beside John, and took his cold, stiff hand in hers, automatically feeling for a pulse, although she knew there wouldn't be one. He had been so frightened of death, so afraid someone would kill him, and it hadn't been a person who had killed him. It had been the elements, and a society that had walked past him, ignoring his plight.

'Any pulse?' Eli asked, his voice gruff, and she shook her head.

'No, nothing,' she said, through a too-tight throat. 'Eli…'

He wasn't listening to her. He was already reaching for John and, when he'd lifted him up into his arms, he walked determinedly towards the ambulance, leaving her where she was, kneeling in the snow.

'If this weather doesn't change soon, I'm afraid we're likely to see more cases like this,' the policeman said sadly. 'And when it's a kid… It always hits hardest.'

'It hits hard no matter who it is,' Brontë replied, thinking of Peg, and the others at Greyfriars. 'And he wasn't just a kid,' she added. 'He had a name, and his name was John. John Smith.'

Wearily, she went to the ambulance but, when she opened the back door, what she saw there stopped her in her tracks. Eli was performing CPR on John. Desperately, and frantically, he was performing CPR.

'Eli…' She bit her lip. 'It's no use. He's been dead for at least two hours.'

'People can survive for longer than that if they're in a state

of suspended animation,' he muttered. 'There are well-doc-
umented cases of people being pulled out of freezing rivers,
and they've been brought back.'

But John hasn't been in a river, she wanted to point out,
but she didn't. Instead, she climbed into the back of the ambulance, closed the door, and began affixing an Ambu bag.

'Epinephrine, and the defibrillator, Brontë,' Eli declared.

Obediently, she did as he asked, though all her professional
knowledge told her neither things would help.

'Set the power to two hundred,' he ordered.

She did, and then she stepped back from the trolley and
closed her eyes. She didn't want to watch this, couldn't bear
to watch this. No power on earth could bring John back, and to
see Eli's stricken face, to watch him frantically do everything
he knew, try everything he could, required more courage than
she possessed.

Three hundred, three hundred and sixty joules… Numbly
she upped the power every time Eli asked her to but, eventually, she knew she had to say something and when, after
twenty minutes, Eli reached for the paddles again, she put her
hand on his arm to stop him.

'He's gone, Eli,' she whispered, her voice breaking. 'We
have to accept he's gone, and nothing we do is going to bring
him back.'

'I can't let him die, Brontë,' he replied, anguish thicken-
ing his voice. 'Maybe if I just keep on trying…if we keep on
shocking him…'

'He's *dead*, Eli,' she said, her voice suspended. 'We're too
late. You have to accept we're too late.'

For a second, she thought he was going to argue with her,
continue with his attempts, then she saw his face twist and,
when he sat down with his head in his hands, she gently kissed
John's cold forehead.

'Be at peace now,' she murmured, fighting to contain her
tears. 'Be at peace, and if there is a heaven be happy there.'

Impotently, she brushed the remaining flakes of snow from his hair. He looked so young, even younger than the fourteen years she'd guessed him to be, and, though she didn't want to do it, she carefully pulled a sheet up over his face, then turned slowly to Eli.

'I always say we can't win them all,' Eli said, his voice muffled. 'That sometimes the only victory we get in this job is if we can manage to keep somebody alive long enough to get them to hospital, and their families can arrive and say goodbye to them, but who was there to say goodbye to John, Brontë? *Who?*'

Instantly, she knelt down in front of him and tentatively covered his hands with her own.

'We were,' she replied. 'We were here, and though we didn't get here in time, I'm sure he knows you tried. You tried so very hard.'

'He ought to have his whole life ahead of him,' Eli exclaimed, raising his eyes to hers, eyes that were full of misery and pain. 'He ought to have a future, a home, a job, and now… Why, Brontë, *why?*'

'I don't know,' she declared. 'I don't know why some people open the wrong door, take the wrong corner.' She glanced over her shoulder at the small, sheet-wrapped figure. 'We'll have to take him to A and E, won't we, so his death can be formally registered?'

Eli nodded. 'And then his details will go to the procurator fiscal who will arrange for an autopsy.'

'Does there have to be one?' she protested. 'He's already been through so much.'

'I'm afraid it's the law. If someone dies unexpectedly, there's always an inquest.' Eli glanced towards the front of their cab, and let out a bitter laugh. 'Guess what, Brontë? Your bosses will be really pleased with ED7 tonight. You made that call in under seven minutes so you can notch John up as one of ED7's success stories even though he's dead.'

'*Don't,*' she begged, hearing the raw pain in his voice. 'Please, *don't*. I know how you're feeling, and this isn't how I wanted his life to end either. Eli—'

He slipped his hands out from under hers, and got to his feet abruptly. 'We'd better get going. There'll be other cases—people who need us.'

'Yes, but…' She scanned his face. 'Eli, I think after we've taken John to the Pentland we should log out, take the rest of the shift off to decompress.'

'I'm fine.'

'You're not,' she insisted. 'I know I'm not, and it's EMDC regulations that when you've had a very difficult job you should come off the road.'

Anger flashed across his face.

'If I say I'm fine, Brontë, then I'm *fine.*'

He wasn't—she knew he wasn't, and neither was she—but she had no opportunity to argue with him. They had scarcely returned to their ambulance after they'd taken John to the Pentland when their MDT flashed up a message.

'Code red. Two-month-old child. Not waking up. Number 108, Nicolson Street.'

'Oh, damn,' Eli muttered, and Brontë felt the same as she put the siren on, and her foot on the accelerator despite the icy, snow-covered road.

It sounded very much like a case of sudden infant death syndrome. Every medic's worst nightmare, every family's worse fear. She hadn't thought this shift could possibly get worse, but it just had, and it got even worse when she reached Nicolson Street, and saw cars parked on either side of the road.

'I know,' she said as Eli opened his mouth. 'This is an emergency, so just park in the middle of the street.'

She did but, even as Eli pulled a medi-bag out of the ambulance, she could hear the sound of people crying from inside number 108. Crying was never a good sign. Crying meant they were probably too late, and they were. One glance at the baby was enough to tell Brontë the child had been dead for quite some time.

'She was all right when I put her to bed,' the young mother sobbed. 'She'd had her bottle, and she was fine—a little snuffly, but nothing else. She was fine, she was fine—and now…'

'I work nights,' her husband declared, rubbing a hand across his tear-stained cheeks, a muscle in his jaw twitching, 'and I just looked in, like I always do when I get home, and Jenny… She was just lying there, and I knew right away there was something wrong.'

Brontë looked helplessly across at Eli, but he was already scooping the baby into his arms.

'Hospital. This little one needs the hospital,' he declared, striding towards the door, and the child's distraught parents grabbed their coats and followed him. 'Blue us in, Brontë.'

Obediently, she hurried out of the house, but she didn't get far. A middle-aged woman was standing beside their ambulance looking distinctly annoyed.

'Look, are you going to be much longer here?' the woman declared. 'I have to get to my night shift at the supermarket, and I can't get past.'

Brontë stared at the woman in stunned disbelief, but Eli wasn't similarly reduced to silence.

'Madam, we have a critical case here,' he replied, 'and it will take as long as it takes.'

'Can't you be a bit more specific, time-wise?' the woman protested, and Eli drew himself up to his full six feet two with an expression on his dark face that would have had Brontë backing away fast.

'Madam, do you have children?' he declared tightly.

'Well, they're teenagers now—'

'Then I'd like to know how you would feel if I couldn't

park outside *your* door because some insensitive, uncaring individual felt I was blocking her way!'

The woman reddened, but she wasn't crushed.

'I want your name!' she exclaimed. 'I demand to know your name so I can make an official complaint!'

'If you can't read the name tag on my uniform, then I'm certainly not going to spell it out for you,' Eli retorted as he got into the back of the ambulance with the baby's parents.

'I'm going to report you—both of you,' the woman yelled after them as Brontë drove away.

Brontë fervently hoped she would. She would enjoy contesting that complaint but, as she drove to the hospital, she would have preferred, even more, to have been anywhere but where she was.

It was one thing to be in A and E when a SIDS baby was brought in, and quite another to drive through the dark Edinburgh Streets with that SIDS baby in the back of her ambulance. She tried not to look in her mirror because she didn't want to see Eli performing CPR on a baby who would never laugh or cry ever again. She tried to stop her ears to the sound of the heartfelt, wrenching sobs from the baby's parents, but she couldn't do that either. All she could do was bite down hard on her lip, and pray she would get to the Pentland fast.

'That was the worst journey of my life,' she mumbled when the baby and its parents had been handed over to the care of the A and E staff.

'I know the regulations say I should have declared the child dead immediately,' Eli replied as he and Brontë left the waiting room, 'but those poor parents…' He shook his head. 'They need to know everything that could be done was done, and in hospital there are people who can help them rather than us just simply driving away, leaving them alone with their baby and their grief.'

He looked as upset as she felt, and she half stretched out her hand to him, only to withdraw it quickly.

'The woman in the street—the one who was complaining,' she said angrily. 'How can people do that, behave like that?'

'It doesn't happen often,' Eli declared. 'In fact, I've watched people park on roundabouts in an attempt to let my ambulance through. I've seen people trying to get themselves into almost impossible spaces so they won't hold me back. I've even scraped the sides of vans as I've tried to get to the hospital as fast as I can, and the drivers have just called after me, "Don't worry about it, mate, it's not important." The vast majority of the public are decent people, Brontë, but some…'

'But *why*?' she insisted. 'Why are some people like that?'

'Because those people live in a "me" world, Brontë. They truly don't care about anyone else, don't think about anyone else's feelings, just take what they want, and concentrate on themselves.'

And he was describing himself, Eli thought with sudden, appalled recognition. No matter how much he tried to deny it, no matter how much he didn't want it to be so, everything Brontë had said about him was true. He *was* arrogant, he *was* self-absorbed, he *was* blind to other people's feelings. How much damage had he inflicted on the women he'd had in his life without noticing it, or—even worse—caring? Okay, so he cared passionately about the homeless, about people who were down on their luck, people who were disadvantaged by circumstances, and society, but in his personal life…

All he'd ever thought about was himself, what he wanted, what made him happy, and he was horrified.

'Are you okay?'

He looked down to see Brontë staring up at him with concern.

'I'm fine—fine.'

'I really do think we should log off,' she said tentatively. 'You need time out—we both do—and—'

'Brontë, I've been doing this job a hell of a lot longer than you have,' he snapped. 'I don't need nannying, I don't need my hand held, so back off, will you?'

She wasn't going to, Brontë decided, as he strode away from her. She'd seen murder in Eli's eyes when the woman in the street had been complaining, and she knew that if she didn't forcibly take him off the road he was going to lose it completely.

'I could do with a coffee,' Eli muttered when Brontë joined him in their ambulance.

'Me, too,' she replied as she drove away from the hospital and turned right at the bottom of the road.

But not at Tony's. They would both have their coffees in their own homes because she was going back to the station and signing them both out whether he liked it or not. Yes, it would leave ED7 one ambulance short but, no matter what Eli said, neither he, nor she, could cope with anything else tonight.

Eli glanced out of the window, then back at her.

'This isn't the quickest way to Tony's.'

'I know.'

'Brontë—'

'We're not going to Tony's,' she continued determinedly, seeing the dawning realisation in his eyes. 'I'm taking us both off the road. No ifs, no buts, no argument,' she added as he swore long and volubly. 'We both need the rest of the shift off.'

'But—'

'My decision, Eli, my call,' she interrupted.

She could feel him fuming beside her, could sense his anger and resentment, but she wasn't going to back down, not even when they got back to ED7, and he got out and slammed the ambulance door with a look at her that would have killed.

'I'll see you tomorrow, then,' she called after him as he began walking away from her, but he didn't reply.

He just kept on walking, and she stared indecisively after him. She'd never seen him looking so low, so down, and part of her wanted to go after him, to say she felt the same way, she understood, and she took a step forward, only to stop.

Distance, Brontë, her mind warned, *you were going to keep your distance, remember?*

But he's so upset, she argued back, and what harm would it do to ask if he'd like some company, to maybe share a meal with her, rather than them both going back to their empty flats alone?

Mistake, Brontë, big mistake, her mind insisted, and for a second she swithered and then before she had even realised she had made a decision she was running across the forecourt after him.

'You're inviting me to your place for a meal?' he said slowly when she caught up with him.

'I just thought… It's been such an awful night…maybe you'd like some company,' she said, feeling her cheeks beginning to heat up under his steady gaze. 'It wouldn't be anything fancy—just what's in the fridge—but the offer's there if…if you want it, that is.'

She thought he was going to refuse—he looked very much as though he intended to—then, to her surprise, he nodded.

'On two conditions,' he said. 'Number one, I drive you home, and number two, we make a short detour to Tony's to pick up some take-away spaghetti and meatballs, and then neither of us have to cook.'

A take-away spaghetti and meatballs sounded wonderful, and it smelled even better when she'd unwrapped it in her small kitchen.

'What do you want to drink?' she asked, taking two plates out of her kitchen cupboard. 'I have a half-bottle of red wine left in the fridge, coffee, tea…?'

'Coffee, as I'm driving,' he replied.

'Comfy seats, and slobbing out in the sitting room?' she said, switching on the kettle. 'Or hard seats with a table in the kitchen?'

'Comfy seats every time,' he declared, and when she led the way into the sitting room he smiled as he gazed around. 'Nice room.'

'The flat's rented, but the furniture's all mine,' she said, pulling a coffee table over. 'It's nothing special, or valuable, just bits and pieces I've picked up from second-hand shops, and car boot sales over the years.'

'You like old furniture?' he said, sitting down on the sofa.

'I like the idea of lots of people having owned something before me,' she said, unzipping her jacket and throwing it over one of the chairs. 'That they've polished something, touched it, maybe left a little bit of themselves, their hearts, in it.' She laughed a little uncertainly. 'And now you're thinking you're having dinner with a fruit cake.'

'A romantic,' he said firmly. 'I think you're a romantic.'

Did he mean that as a compliment, or a condemnation? She wasn't sure and nor was she about to ask.

'I'll see if the kettle's boiled,' she said instead. 'Don't wait for me—just start eating.'

He hadn't, she noticed when she returned to the sitting room. He'd taken off his jacket, but he was still sitting where she'd left him, lost in thought and, as she stood in the doorway, holding their coffees, a lump came to her throat. He looked so tired. Tired, and beaten, and she wanted to put down the coffees, and take him in her arms and say, 'I'll make everything all right,' but she couldn't. She couldn't make everything all right tonight, nobody could.

'Thought I told you to eat?' she said, all cheerleader bright, and he turned to face her with an effort.

'Sorry,' he replied. 'I was miles away.'

'Someone—a man who isn't always the smartest of men—once told me, Don't think,' she observed. 'And, on this occasion, I think he was right.'

Eli forced a smile. 'So, I'm a dummkopf now, too, am I, along with all my other faults?'

'Hey, why should I be the only one with a gazillion labels?' she protested, taking a seat opposite him, hating to see that forced smile on his lips. 'And you're not a dummkopf, just a very complicated man, and now eat something.'

'Yes, ma'am,' he replied, giving her a mock salute, and she managed to laugh, and picked up her knife and fork because she knew if she didn't she would put her arms round him anyway.

Because she didn't simply want to comfort him, she wanted him. Even though it would end in heartbreak, even though it would never be for ever, she knew she still wanted him, and she always would.

'Great meatballs,' she said, deliberately putting some in her mouth.

'Yup,' he said. 'I was wondering… Tomorrow's your last day at the station, so…'

'You can tell everyone at ED7 I'm giving the station a glowing report,' she answered, and he shook his head.

'That's not what I meant. I was wondering what you were going to do, whether you were going to stick with this job, or…'

'I think we've pretty well established I'm rubbish at it.' She smiled. 'So when I hand in my report, I'll also be handing in my resignation.'

He sat back in his seat, his face concerned. 'Christmas is a lousy time to be out of work.'

'Maybe one of the big stores will be looking for a spare pixie, or an elf, for their Santa grotto,' she declared. 'Having said which, I'd have to lose a bit of weight first. Pixies and elves tend to be slender.'

'You look perfect to me.'

Her gaze met his, then she looked away fast. Oh, hell. Why did he have to have such intense blue eyes? Why couldn't he have had ordinary eyes, eyes which didn't make her heart jump around so much in her chest?

'You've just broken one of your promises,' she said, mock stern as she determinedly took another fork of spaghetti. 'The no-flattery one.'

'I wasn't flattering you.'

Oh, double hell. Change the subject, Brontë, she told herself, and change it fast, but she couldn't think of a single thing to say, and he raised an eyebrow.

'Cat got your tongue?'

'Nope,' she replied. 'Just enjoying the food. As my mother used to say—'

She bit off the rest of what she'd been about to say. Mothers were not a good topic, not with Eli, and he clearly sensed her discomfort because he smiled a little wryly.

'What you said—about going to an agency to try to find my mother,' he began, and she cut across him fast.

'I'm sorry, I should never have suggested that. I can fully understand why you wouldn't want to go down that road—'

'I already have. I went to an agency two years ago because I thought...' He sighed. 'I don't know what I thought. Maybe I was looking for closure like you said, or maybe I just wanted to ask her, face-to-face, why she left me.'

'Did...did you find her?' she said hesitantly, not really wanting to know, but knowing she had to ask.

'I was too late. She... She died six months before I started my enquiries.'

Nothing could have prepared her for him revealing that, and nothing could have prepared her for the bleakness she could see in his face.

'Oh, Eli, I am sorry,' she said softly, 'so very, very sorry.'

'She took her reasons for leaving me to the grave, so now I'll never know why she did it,' he murmured, his eyes dark. 'Maybe if I was a "think the best of people" person like you, I could pretend. I could create a scenario, a perfect resolution, but I'm not like you.'

'You don't have to be,' she said, hating to see the pain in his eyes, wanting so much to ease it, but not knowing how, 'but I do think you need to let it go, or it will never stop hurting you.'

'Yeah, well… Sorry,' he added, 'I've really put a dampener on our dinner, haven't I?'

'I'm just flattered you felt you could tell me,' she said, and saw one corner of his mouth turn up in an attempt at a smile which didn't deceive her for a second.

'I thought you said flattery was a no-no?' he pointed out.

'Oh, very funny,' she said, 'now eat before all this lovely sauce gets cold.'

He did, and she did, too, but as they ate she knew she could have been eating anything for all the impression it was making because all she was aware of was him. Him sitting in her sitting room, him just an arm's stretch away from her. Every time he pushed his hair back from his forehead, she thought, *Let me do that, I want to do that.* Every time he moved in his seat she tensed, hopeful, expectant.

Stop it, Brontë, she told herself, *stop it.* He's just a man, just a very handsome man, but he wasn't just a man, and she knew he wasn't.

'Something wrong?' he asked, looking up and catching her gaze on him.

'No—absolutely not,' she said brightly, much too brightly, and, because she was nervous, she forked up too much spaghetti only to watch in dismay as some of it dropped off her fork and landed with a soft splat on the front of her shirt.

'You are a klutz, aren't you?' Eli chuckled. 'No, don't

stand up,' he added as she made to do just that, 'you'll get it on the carpet.'

And before she realised what he was going to do, he had picked up his napkin, and begun wiping the sauce and spaghetti from her shirt.

And it was torture. The most exquisite form of torture as he wiped down the front of her shirt in a smooth, rhythmic movement, and she felt his fingers through the napkin, through the material of her shirt, hot on her breast, and she knew when he caught his breath because hers caught at exactly the same moment.

'I think…' She heard him swallow. 'I think you're respectable again.'

Slowly she raised her eyes to his.

'Am I?'

Even to her own ears her voice sounded husky, and she saw him crumple the napkin into a tight ball.

'I shouldn't have done that, and I think…I think I should go now,' he said.

She didn't want him to go. She didn't want him to leave. She wanted him, and it didn't matter to her any more if she could only have this one night with him. It didn't even matter if he whispered words he didn't mean, said exactly the same things to her that he'd said to dozens of other women. She had no pride left. She just wanted him.

'You don't have to go,' she said, saw his pupils darken, then he got to his feet fast, shaking his head.

'Brontë, I do. You want more than I can give—you know you do—and you deserve more.'

She stood, too, and, before he could evade her, she put her hands on his chest, and felt his rapid heartbeat.

'Right now, I want you,' she said softly. 'No strings, no promises, I just want you.'

'Brontë—'

She silenced him by standing up on her toes, and kissing

him, with no reserve, no holding back, exactly as she'd kissed him in the snow what seemed—oh—like a lifetime ago now, felt him hesitate for a heartbeat, and then he was holding her tight, and kissing her back with a desperate, urgent need.

Heat, all she could feel was a pulsing, throbbing heat, and when he pulled her shirt free from her combat trousers, and slid his hand up underneath it to cup and stroke her breast, she shuddered against him, wanting more, so much more.

'Brontë, think about this,' he groaned as her fingers fumbled with his shirt buttons while she planted a row of kisses along his collarbone.

'I have,' she said, pulling his shirt apart so she could look at him, could see his beauty, his strength. 'And I have never been more certain of anything in my life.'

And she wasn't, she thought, as she claimed his lips again, and felt him slide her shirt down off her shoulders, felt her bra go in an instant, and then she heard his sharp intake of breath.

'I could kill the man who did this to you,' he said, his voice tight, vicious, as he stared at the ugly scar on her chest, but, when her hands instinctively came up to cover herself, he caught them, and pressed a kiss into each palm. 'He hurt you. He made you afraid, and I don't want you ever to be hurt, or afraid, again.'

And you'll hurt me so much more when you go, she thought, but she didn't say those words.

'Just make love to me, Eli,' she whispered instead. 'That's all I want and need right now—just for you to make love to me.'

And somehow they made it to her bedroom, and soon their clothes were gone, and they were skin to skin, on her bed, his body hard and muscular against her, and his kisses weren't enough, his touch wasn't nearly enough.

But he was hesitating still, she knew it, sensed it, knew he was holding himself back, and she knew why, and she kissed him harder, with greater intensity, and reached down to stroke him, stroke him, until he gasped under her fingers, and it was then he slid into her, hot, and hard, balancing himself on his elbows, his eyes fixed on her.

And he said her name, and it sounded almost like an apology, but she didn't want an apology. She arched herself up against him, forcing him on, so that he slid even deeper into her, and she bit her lip as he began rocking into her, over and over again, and she could feel it coming, feel the blood surging to her fingertips, her toes, every part of her, knew she was reaching the precipice, and she wrapped her legs round him, drawing him further inside her, and then she broke. Broke and began spiralling and shaking beneath him, and he came, too, and as he did, he laid his head between her breasts and she heard him give a sigh that was almost a groan.

CHAPTER SEVEN

Sunday, 9:30 a.m.

ELI lay on his back and smiled as he gazed down at Brontë. She was lying curled up against his side, her head resting against his chest, and gently he placed a kiss on top of her head, and tightened his hold on her.

Last night had been the most incredible night of his life. He'd made love to her twice, and each time it had been wonderful, but that second time... That second time had been special. Slower, less frantic, it had been like nothing he had ever experienced before. It had felt almost as though he had come home which was crazy because he'd never had a home, not a proper one, but Brontë had taken him somewhere he'd never been before, and it was somewhere he didn't want to leave, not ever.

She stirred in his arms, almost as though she had read his mind, then she stretched against him, her full breasts rubbing lightly against his ribcage, sending a tremor of arousal through him, and his smile widened as she opened her eyes.

'Morning, sleepyhead,' he said.

For a second, she looked confused, as though she wasn't a hundred per cent certain where she was, then her grey eyes softened for an instant, and then, just as quickly, she looked away, and suddenly—and unaccountably—he felt cold.

'What time is it?' she asked.

Was it his imagination, or did her voice sound carefully neutral? Unconsciously, he shook his head. Imagination, it must be his imagination. He knew he had pleased her last night. Hell, just thinking about the tiny cries, and sighs, she'd given was enough to turn him on all over again.

'Nine-thirty,' he replied. 'Which means we have a whole day ahead of us before work tonight. A whole day in which we can do whatever we want, and I've already thought of some pretty interesting things we can do. For example...'

Gently, he slid his hand up her side and began brushing his fingers across one of her nipples. It hardened instantly but, when he moved to the other breast, she eased herself out of his arms, and moved further away from him in the bed.

'I'm afraid I have plans for today,' she said. 'Things to do, places to go and a report on ED7 to write.'

'If you need to go shopping, I can carry your bags, and as for the report, I can help you there, too,' he said, reaching out to cup her chin only to see her turn her head away.

'You can't help me,' she replied. 'The things I need to do... Only I can do them.'

'Okay.' He nodded, regrouping quickly. 'How about I keep you supplied with coffees all day, then rustle you up a delicious lunch, followed by an equally jaw-dropping dinner? You have to eat, and if you've got someone like me who—' he grinned '—is not only good in the bedroom, but also pretty damn good when it comes to wielding a saucepan, why not use me?'

'Today's not a good day for me, Eli,' she muttered. 'I've made plans—plans I can't cancel.'

'Then what about tomorrow—or the day after?' he said, feeling a chill begin to creep around his heart. 'I'll be on a three-day break because I'll just have finished a seven-day block, and if you're handing in your resignation I can check out Santa grottoes with you to make sure you don't end up working with a load of licentious pixies.'

She didn't laugh—she didn't even smile—and she still wasn't looking at him, he noticed.

'Actually, I thought I might go and stay with my sister for the next few days,' she declared.

'But, Brontë, you don't even *like* your sister,' he replied, and she shrugged.

'Yes, well, she's still family.'

If it had been anyone else he would have said he was getting the brush-off, but this was Brontë. Brontë who didn't play games, didn't toy with other people's emotions, so the fault had to be his, and he sat up, tucking the duvet round her so she wouldn't get cold.

'Brontë, listen to me,' he said. 'I don't know what I did wrong last night—'

'You didn't do anything wrong,' she broke in. 'It was great, just great, but I'm leaving ED7 today—'

'Which doesn't mean we can't see each other any more,' he protested. 'It doesn't mean this has to end.'

He saw her fingers grip the sheet.

'Eli, I had a great time last night—fabulous, truly—but can't we just leave it at that?'

'Leave it at that?' he echoed. 'Brontë, in case you've forgotten, we made love last night, and I think we should at least talk about it. I've obviously upset you in some way—'

'You haven't—not in the least. Look, as you told me before,' she continued as he tried to interrupt, 'there's mediocre sex, okay sex and great sex, and though the sex last night was pretty good, my feeling is we should quit while we're ahead, shake hands, wish each other well, and move on.'

They should shake hands and wish each other well? They'd had great sex, but they should quit while they were ahead?

She was making what they'd shared sound so clinical, so

unemotional, and it hadn't been like that, at least not for him, and he caught hold of her chin with his fingers, and forced her to look up at him.

'Brontë, *talk* to me. Don't give me all these platitudes, all this…this crap. *Talk* to me.'

'I would if there was anything left to say,' she replied, her eyes meeting his briefly, then skittering away. 'We had a great time, but can't you just accept that's all it was? Now, do you want to use the shower first? I don't want to hurry you—make you feel I'm throwing you out or anything—but…'

She was throwing him out. No ifs, no buts, she was throwing him out, and he didn't want to be thrown out. He wanted to hold her. Not even to make love to her again, though his body would have welcomed that with unbridled enthusiasm; he just wanted to hold her, to try to recapture that wonderful feeling of belonging he'd experienced last night.

'Brontë—'

'So are you showering first? It's just, like I said, I have—'

'Things to do, people to see and a report to write,' he finished for her grimly. 'Fine. Absolutely fine.' He threw back the duvet, and stood. 'Do I get a cup of coffee before I go, or would that interrupt your schedule too much?'

'You know where the kitchen is,' Brontë replied.

And she turned on her side when she said it, so all he could see of her was her bare back which meant she was well and truly shutting him out.

Well, fine, he thought, angrily. If that's what she wanted, then that was just *fine*, and he walked out of the bedroom, and slammed the door and didn't see Brontë bury her face deep in her pillow so he wouldn't be able to see or hear her tears.

'I don't see anyone,' Brontë declared when she turned into Richmond Street. '"Elderly woman lying in the street," Dispatch said, but I can't see anyone.'

'Drive to the top of the road, then come back down again,' Eli replied.

It was on the tip of her tongue to say, 'And, like, *duh*, so you didn't think I was going to think of that?' but she didn't.

Perky, and upbeat, Brontë, she told herself. You are going to be perky and upbeat for the whole of this shift if it kills you, and quickly she drove up Richmond Street, then back down again.

'Well, unless she's the invisible woman,' she declared, 'I'd say she's either just wandered off, or it was a hoax call.'

'Someone's waving to us from outside that house,' Eli said suddenly. 'Pull over.'

Obediently, Brontë did as he'd said, and an Indian gentleman walked gingerly over the snow towards them.

'Are you looking for the lady who fell?' he asked, and when Brontë nodded he looked a little awkward, a little guilty.

'She is in my house. I know you are not supposed to move someone who is hurt,' he added as Eli sucked in his breath, 'but it is so cold out here, and my wife, Indira, she said we couldn't leave her, not in the snow, not when she was clearly in such pain. My name is Mr Shafi, by the way.'

'That was very kind of you, Mr Shafi,' Brontë said quickly before Eli could say what she knew he was itching to say. 'Can you tell us anything about her?' she continued, as she reached for a medi-bag.

'Her name is Violet Swanson,' he replied, ushering Brontë towards his home. 'The poor old lady... She had been to the chapel, to say her prayers, and she slipped on the snow on her way home. Indira...she thinks perhaps the lady's arm is broken.'

Violet Swanson's arm *was* broken, and she was clearly in considerable pain.

'So stupid,' she murmured. 'Such a stupid, stupid thing to have done. I know I should have waited until morning to go to church, but it's very peaceful there at night, very comforting.'

'You'll have to go to hospital,' Eli declared. 'I'm sorry, but you really must,' he added when Violet Swanson began to argue. 'That arm needs to be X-rayed, and put in plaster. Is there anyone you'd like us to contact, to say where we're taking you?'

'I'm a widow, dear, live on my own,' Violet Swanson replied, wincing sharply, as Brontë began to strap her arm across her chest to keep it secure. 'No family. Archie and I were never blessed, but then you don't always get what you want out of life, do you, so you just have to make the best of things.'

Which is what I'm going to do, Brontë thought, deliberately avoiding Eli's eyes. Last night... It had been the most wonderful night of her life, but she'd known it was just that. One night. One incredible night she would be able to look back on, and remember, and though she'd remember it with some pain—the pain of knowing he was the man she wanted, but could never have—it was better to walk away now than live with Eli for two months and then have him leave. That, she knew, she would never survive.

'Mrs Swanson, do you think you can walk?' she asked. 'We have a carry-chair—'

'Of course I can walk,' Violet protested, but from the way she swayed when she stood, it was patently obvious that not only was she in a lot more pain than she was admitting, her whole system had taken a severe shock.

'The carry-chair,' Eli said firmly.

'Thank you for helping,' Brontë told Mr Shafi and his wife, as she helped Mrs Swanson into the chair. 'It was very kind of you.'

The man shrugged. 'What else could we do? We could not leave the poor lady, turn our backs on her.'

A lot of people could, Brontë thought when they'd got

Mrs Swanson safely settled in the back of the ambulance, and she set off for the Pentland. In fact, too many people did. Too many people walked on by, thinking, Someone else's problem, not mine.

'It's a pity there's not a lot more people in the world like that nice couple in Richmond Street,' she observed after they had delivered Mrs Swanson to A and E. 'People who are willing to put themselves out, to help others.'

'To be fair, some people prefer to keep themselves to themselves,' Eli replied. 'They don't want to let down their guard in case people encroach on their personal space.'

Like me, he thought, as he watched Brontë climb back into the ambulance. Always he had been the one who'd been in control in all of his relationships, the one who had decided when it was over, but this time...

For the first time in his life he was completely out of his depth. For the first time in his life he didn't know what to do. Maybe if he talked to Brontë again. Maybe if he waited until the end of this shift, then talked to her...

And said what? his mind asked.

That he didn't want her to walk right out of his life. That he wanted to spend time with her. A lot more time. That he'd miss her snippiness, and her laughter. He'd miss her silver-grey eyes, and her fringe which never would stay flat. He'd miss *her.*

But how could he get her back? His looks had always been his primary tool of seduction. His looks, and some well-practised flattery and flirtation, but none of that would get him anywhere with Brontë. He needed something else, and he would have to find it fast or she would walk right out of his life just as quickly as she'd walked into it.

'Code red. Male, aged twenty, collapsed and in pain. Number 82, Bristol Street,' the MDT screen read, and Brontë grimaced slightly.

Code red sounded ominous, but Eli hadn't said to switch

on the siren. Actually, Eli hadn't said very much at all since they'd come on duty, but he was watching her, she knew he was. Watching her with a slightly puzzled expression in his eyes, as though he was trying to figure something out. She wished he wouldn't. She wished he would just take what she'd said this morning at face value, because it would be easier for both of them if he did.

Will it? her heart whispered as she drove down Melrose Street. *Will it really?*

It had to be, she told herself, because the alternative was so much worse.

'Turn left at the bottom of the road for Bristol Street,' Eli advised and, as she did, she blinked as she saw the row of elegant Georgian buildings.

'Whoa, but these houses are seriously stunning.' She gasped. 'I wouldn't be able to afford to live here even on a hundred times my income.'

'Money can't buy you happiness, or contentment,' Eli replied cryptically.

He was right. Number 82, Bristol Street might have been just as lavish inside as it was out, but its occupants weren't in the least to be envied.

'You the ambulance dudes?' a young man asked, his voice distinctly slurred as he opened the front door.

'Yes, we're the ambulance dudes.' Eli sighed. 'Where's the casualty?'

The young man waved his hand vaguely. 'Dining room, I think. Or it could be the sitting room. Dunno, really.'

'Great,' Eli muttered, pushing past him. 'Let's hope somebody in this house is in a fit state to answer some questions.'

Brontë very much doubted it. That the son, or daughter, of the house had decided to throw a party was clear. She could hear the thumping sound of music and laughter, and there was discarded food, and empty bottles, scattered everywhere.

'I wonder where the parents are?' she asked as she followed Eli over the parquet entrance hall, feeling her boots stick with every step.

'Winter cruise, shooting in the highlands, down in London to take in a few exhibitions?' Eli suggested, and Brontë shook her head.

'You'd think they'd have more sense than to go off and leave a bunch of youngsters with no supervision. So, what do we do?' she continued. 'Search every room, or what?'

They didn't have to. A girl who couldn't have been more than eighteen appeared, looking scared and worried.

'Gavin's through here,' she said, pointing to a door at the end of the hallway. 'He's acting all funny—not making any sense at all.'

Brontë wasn't surprised when she saw the young man. He was lying on a sofa, curled up into a ball, clutching his stomach and moaning, but it was the rest of his appearance which told her immediately what the problem was. His pupils were almost pinpoints, his skin was clammy, his fingernails and lips had a bluish tinge, and he was twitching uncontrollably.

'What's he taken?' Eli said, as he crouched down beside the young man.

'A few beers—maybe a shot or two of whisky,' the girl replied, and Eli exhaled with irritation.

'Look, give me credit for some sense,' he declared as Brontë began strapping a blood pressure cuff to the young man's arm. 'Is it crystal meth, cocaine, Ecstasy, or heroin?'

'Gavin doesn't do drugs,' the young girl protested. 'He's just had a bit too much to drink, that's all.'

'Sweetheart, he clearly doesn't know where he is, or even *who* he is, and you don't get muscle spasticity like that from booze,' Eli protested. 'So, I'm going to ask you again. What's he taken?'

'Eli, his BP is way too low, and his pulse is very weak,'

Brontë murmured. 'We're going to have to tube him, and fast.'

'Did you hear that?' Eli demanded, and the young woman looked from Brontë to the young man in panic.

'I…I don't know anything,' she said.

'Look, what's your name?' Brontë asked, seeing Eli shake his head in despair.

'It's Joanna,' the young woman replied. 'My name's Joanna.'

'Joanna, Gavin is very sick indeed,' Brontë said, 'and, without wanting to frighten you, he could die. We need to know what he's taken so we know how to treat him,' she continued as the young girl let out a gasp, and tears filled her eyes. 'We're not here to make judgements, but to *help*.'

'My parents will kill me,' Joanna whispered. 'They don't know about this party, and when they find out…'

Out of the corner of her eye, Brontë could see Eli was beginning to insert an intubation tube into Gavin's trachea to help him breathe, but they needed to know what the young man had taken, and they needed to know it fast.

'Joanna, has Gavin had any seizures?' she asked.

'Seizures?' Joanna repeated blankly.

'Had a fit, thrashed about at all?' Brontë explained.

The girl nodded. 'He had one about half an hour ago.'

'Please, Joanna,' Brontë said softly. 'We need to know what Gavin's taken before it's too late.'

The girl bit her lip, then took a shuddering breath.

'Heroin,' she said, her voice thick. 'He's taken some heroin.'

'Do you know how much?' Brontë said, and the young woman shook her head.

'Brendan… He said it would make Gavin feel great. He's been feeling a bit down, you see. His parents have stopped his allowance because he crashed his dad's Mercedes, and it was just meant to pep him up a bit.'

Eli muttered something under his breath that was most definitely unprintable.

'How often has he taken heroin?' he demanded.

'I think this was the first time,' Joanna replied, 'but I don't know. I honestly and truly don't know.'

'Brontë, his BP is going down even more,' Eli said urgently. 'We have to go.'

'Can I come, too?' the girl asked. 'He's my sort of boyfriend, you see.'

A sort of boyfriend who might not survive the night, Brontë thought, as she helped Eli carry Gavin out to the ambulance, past youngsters who were still partying, apparently oblivious—or uncaring—about what was happening in front of them.

'Do you think he'll pull through?' Brontë asked after they had taken Gavin to the Pentland.

'We can but hope,' Eli replied, 'but the waste, Brontë, the damn waste of a young life, if he doesn't!'

'I know.' She sighed. 'All that money, all those advantages, and yet to be so stupid.'

'Yeah, well, I'm afraid all the money in the world doesn't buy you some plain, old-fashioned common sense.' Eli glanced down at his watch and sighed. 'And can you believe we've only been on duty for a couple of hours?'

Brontë couldn't. This shift felt endless, and it was about to get worse, she thought when a message appeared on their MDT.

'Gang fight in Princes Street Gardens. Police in attendance. All available ambulances to attend the incident. Repeat, all available ambulances to attend, and offer assistance.'

Her stomach lurched. A gang fight. That meant a crowd, and she was being asked to drive there, to get out amongst it, to offer help.

'Brontë…'

She heard the instant concern in Eli's voice, the gentle

understanding, and breathed in again, hoping it might work, but it didn't.

'I'm okay,' she lied, hating the betraying wobble in her voice as she switched on the ignition. 'I'll…I'll be okay.'

She wouldn't be, she knew she wouldn't. Already her heart was racing at just the thought of being amongst a crowd, and her palms were so sweaty she could barely grip the steering wheel.

Failure, her heart whispered, *you're a failure. People could be hurt out there, and you can't do anything to help them.*

She wondered what Eli was thinking. *Liability,* that's what he was probably thinking, that he was stuck with a liability. Well, at least she would get him there fast, she determined. At least he wouldn't be able to accuse her of deliberately dawdling, but it was easier said than done.

'Look, I know you don't want to go there—that crowds freak you out—but couldn't you drive just a little faster,' he said softly, and Brontë glanced at him helplessly.

'It isn't me. I've got my foot to the floor, but we're losing power, and I don't know why.'

'You did make sure she was filled up?' he said, only to smile a little ruefully when Brontë shot him a withering glance. 'Sorry. Stupid question. The trouble is she's old, clapped out.'

'What do you want me to do?' Brontë asked. 'We're not going to be much use ferrying casualties to hospital at this speed, and what if it breaks down on the way to the Pentland with a seriously hurt person in the back?'

Eli chewed his lip indecisively, then seemed to come to a decision.

'Get as close to Princes Street Gardens as you can. At least that way I can be of use, help the other paramedics.'

And they looked as though they could do with all the help they could get, Brontë thought when she reached the garden and saw not just an array of police cars, and ambulances, but a seething mass of fighting youths.

'Stay where you are,' Eli ordered as he pulled a medi-bag out from behind him, and opened his passenger door. 'When I get out, lock all the doors, call Dispatch and tell them we have a problem with the ambulance, and stay where you are.'

'But—'

'Keep the MDT display on, and if anything urgent comes in, try and attract one of the policemen's attention, but do *not* get out of the ambulance.'

'But, Eli—'

He was gone before she could say anything else and, for one brief moment, she saw him clearly, pushing his way through the fighting youths, head and shoulders taller than most of them, and then he was gone and she wrapped her arms around herself as a wave of nausea engulfed her.

Never had she felt so frightened. She could see the rival gangs quite clearly through her windscreen. Some were hurling stones, some were armed with bits of wood they'd clearly torn from garden fences, some were simply using their fists, and here and there, she saw the flash of metal in the moonlight. Knives. Some of them were armed with knives.

And the fight was moving closer to her now. Occasionally, somebody was thrown against the ambulance, and she could feel it shaking under the impact, could hear the thud of the body, see wild, enraged faces in front of her, and the noise… the noise…

She put her hands over her ears, and curled herself into a ball in the driver's seat, but it didn't help. She could still hear the oaths, the roars, the screams, and she wanted to put the ambulance into reverse, to get away, but even if the ambulance would go anywhere, Eli was out there, amongst all the mayhem, and he might need help, except she couldn't help him, she couldn't do anything but sit here, with her eyes tight shut, and wait.

A bottle crashing against her windscreen had her sitting bolt upright in panic. They couldn't get in, surely none of them could get in, and then—out of the corner of her eye— she saw something else. A young boy was lying beside one of the hedges. A young boy, with an ashen face, and closed eyes, who didn't look much older than John Smith had been. A young boy who had blood on his forehead, and blood drip- ping down from his fingers onto the snow below.

Desperately she scanned the melee in front of her. If she could just see a paramedic—any paramedic—maybe she could attract their attention, point out the boy, but all she could see was people fighting, The blood dripping from the boy's hand was forming a pool, and he was even whiter now than he'd been a minute ago. He was going to die. She knew as surely as she knew anything that he was going to die, all alone with no one to help him, and a sob broke from her.

Somewhere in the distance someone screamed, and she bit down hard on her lip until she tasted blood. If she'd been there when John had been dying she could have saved him, but she hadn't been there. She was here now, though, and that young boy lying so close to her needed her, and she could help him if she could only find the courage.

With shaking hands she dragged a medi-bag out from behind her, and took a shuddering breath. She could do this. She *had* to do this and, though her heart was pounding, she opened the ambulance door and got out.

Where the hell was she? Eli wondered, as he scanned the now almost deserted gardens. He'd told her to stay in the ambulance, not to move, but perhaps she'd got so frightened she'd just taken off into the night which meant she could be anywhere.

'You've not seen Brontë O'Brian, have you?' Eli asked urgently as one of the paramedics from ED12 passed him.

'Small, golden-brown hair, big grey eyes? The government number cruncher.'

The paramedic shook his head.

'Mate, I doubt whether I would have recognised my own mother in that mob tonight. Bedlam. Sheer bedlam.' He glanced over his shoulder. 'Maybe one of the cops might have seen her.'

Eli nodded, and quickly hurried over to the small group of policemen who were standing by one of the railings, looking decidedly the worse for wear. One had a black eye, the other's uniform was torn, and one had a badly cut lip.

'I'm looking for my colleague,' Eli declared. 'Small woman, short golden-brown hair, big grey eyes. Have you seen her at all?'

'Can't say I have,' the policeman with the black eye replied. 'Maybe she went off in one of the ambulances?'

It was a possibility—a remote one—but a possibility, but as Eli turned to go, the policeman with the cut lip suddenly frowned.

'A small woman, you said?' he declared. 'With short, golden-brown hair?'

'That's her,' Eli said eagerly. 'Do you know where she is?'

'If it's the same woman you're talking about, I'm afraid she took a knife wound. Pretty serious, too, by the looks of it.'

Eli's heart clutched in his chest. A knife wound. Pretty serious.

No. No. *No.*

If she was badly hurt, if she was… No, he couldn't think that—wouldn't allow himself to think that—but he had to know, had to find out.

'Can you take me to the hospital?' he said.

'Sure thing, mate,' the policeman with the black eye replied. 'Which one?'

The Pentland, or the Waverley? Eli desperately tried to think, but his brain didn't seem to be working. All he could see was Brontë lying white, and cold, and bleeding, on the snow. Brontë slipping away from him on a sterile hospital trolley, without him, and him never being able to say what he knew now to be the truth. That the indefinable emotion he experienced every time he was near her, was love. The feelings of protectiveness, the need, and the rightness, he had felt last night, was love. It was an emotion he had told Brontë didn't exist. An emotion he had denied for the past thirty-four years, and he couldn't lose it now. Simply couldn't.

'Hey, mate, you okay?' one of the policemen asked as Eli dashed a hand across his eyes.

'Yes, I'm…I'm okay,' Eli replied, trying to blot out the image of Brontë lying on a cold mortuary slab. 'Can we go now?'

'No problem,' the policeman replied, but as Eli turned to follow him he saw a figure emerging from the gardens.

A figure, whose short pixie cut was sticking up all over the place. A figure who had a smear of blood on her cheek, and who looked exhausted, and before he even realised he was moving, Eli was running towards her, his arms outstretched, and when he reached her, he clasped her into his arms and enveloped her in a crushing embrace.

'Don't ever do that to me again,' he said, his voice breaking. 'Don't ever just disappear like that, not *ever*. When I got back to the ambulance and you weren't there…'

'I couldn't stay,' she mumbled into his chest. 'There was this young boy, and he reminded me so much of John, and I couldn't stay, just couldn't, and…' She raised her head to him, her eyes shining. 'I did it, Eli. I *did it*. I was terrified, and I thought I was going to faint—'

'Are you okay?' he interrupted, scanning her face. 'The blood on your cheek—is it yours?'

'No—no—it's someone else's,' she said dismissively, 'but

did you hear me, Eli? I conquered my fear. After I'd treated the boy, I just kept going, and going, with other casualties, and I could do it, I could *do it*!'

'This past half-hour,' he murmured, not really listening to her, 'when I couldn't find you, and the policeman said someone looking like you had been taken to hospital—'

'That was Liz Logan from ED10. She got a nasty knife wound. I saw them take her away, but I think she's going to be okay because she was talking…' Brontë chuckled. 'Actually, she was swearing.'

Eli held her tighter. 'Do you have *any* idea how scared I was when I thought it was you?'

'You worry too much.'

'And you…' The relief he had felt at finding her safe turned to anger as he remembered the agonies he'd been through, fearing the worst. 'What the hell did you think you were doing? I *told* you to stay in the cab. Didn't I tell you to stay there, but, no, Brontë O'Brian thinks she knows best, so out she gets, completely disobeying my order….'

She pulled herself out of his arms, and glared up at him.

'Order? You didn't give me any order. You just suggested I should stay in the ambulance, but, Eli, it was mayhem out there—'

'All the more reason for you to stay put.'

'—and people were hurt, bleeding. I couldn't ignore them, and keep my self-respect, and once I got outside, once I started treating people, I was fine, I was okay. I *am* fine, I *am* okay.'

'I'm *not*,' he said with feeling. 'Brontë, get in the ambulance.'

'There's no point,' she protested. 'It's not going anywhere until the breakdown truck arrives.'

'No, but we have an audience,' Eli declared, suddenly becoming aware that the three policemen were watching them with various grins on their faces. 'And I have more to say to you.'

'More to chew me out for, you mean.' Brontë sighed. 'Don't you see what this means for me, Eli? It means I can be a nurse again, go back to doing what I love most. Or I could retrain, become a paramedic. Not at ED7, of course,' she added quickly. 'I wouldn't inflict myself on you—'

'I wouldn't mind.'

'But the big thing—the most important thing—is you said I'd get over my fear, and you were right, so, please…' She caught and held his gaze anxiously. 'Can't you be pleased for me?'

'I am pleased for you.' He nodded. 'But I still want you to get in the ambulance.'

'But—'

He wasn't taking any buts. He took her by the arm and steered her firmly towards the ambulance, and waited until she'd got in before he climbed into the passenger seat beside her.

'Look, I'm sorry you were worried,' she said immediately. 'I should have left a note or something—'

'Brontë…' He paused, and shook his head. 'You scared the living daylights out of me, but, believe me, what I'm going to say now is a hell of a lot more frightening.'

'Something's happened to one of the paramedics?' she said instantly. 'Liz Logan, she was hurt a lot more badly than we thought—'

'No, it's not Liz, or any of the other paramedics,' he interrupted. 'This…this is about me.'

'You,' she said with a frown. 'I'm sorry, but I don't understand.'

'I don't either,' he murmured with a wry and rueful smile, 'and, as I've never said this to anyone before, I'm probably going to mess it up big time.'

'Mess what up?' she declared in confusion. 'Eli, you're not making any sense.'

'I don't think I have since the first minute I met you,' he said slowly. 'You see...when I thought I might never see you again...when I thought I might have lost you for good... It was then I realised you're the most irritating, annoying, lippy, wonderful woman I've ever met, and I need you in my life.'

She blinked. 'Okay, I understood the annoying and the lippy part, but as for the rest...'

'I'm saying I love you, Brontë O'Brian.'

She didn't say anything. She simply stared at him blankly, and he felt his cheeks darken with colour. Surely he couldn't have got it so badly wrong? He thought—he was sure—she felt something for him, but maybe he'd been wrong.

'Aren't you going to say anything?' he said with an attempt at a smile that fooled neither of them.

'I'm waiting for the punchline,' she declared. 'What you just said... There's got to be a punchline.'

'No punchline.'

'But...' She shook her head. 'Eli, you've only known me for seven days, and for most of that time we've shouted at each other, and you don't believe in love. You told me you didn't.'

'I didn't until I met you,' he said awkwardly. 'I've never wanted any woman to stay with me forever, but I want you to.'

'Is this another pitch?' she said, and he saw her lip tremble. 'Eli, if this is another of your pitches, another of your lines, I swear I will never forgive you.'

Never had he regretted his reputation as much as he did now when he saw tears shimmering in her eyes. Never had he so much regretted all the women he had dated, and then so carelessly discarded.

'No—absolutely *not*!' he exclaimed, reaching out to

capture one of her hands in his. 'I wish I knew the words to say to convince you I'm telling you the truth. Brontë, I *love* you. I have never said that to a woman before, and I know I will never say it to any other woman. I love you, and I know I always will.'

'Is this about last night?' she said uncertainly. 'Because we slept together, you now feel guilty—'

'*No!*' He let go of her hand, and gripped her shoulders. 'Last night…last night you gave me something I've never had before. It wasn't simply sex,' he continued as she tried to interrupt. 'I've had enough sex to know the difference. It's not something I'm proud of, it's something I now bitterly regret—all the women I hurt without even realising I was hurting them—but I can't erase my past, can't change it.'

'Eli—'

'I told you once before you're one of a kind, Brontë O'Brian, and you are. Last night… Last night you made me feel whole, you made me feel complete, that I finally belonged, and I want you to stay with me for always, to marry me. If…' His eyes met hers. 'If you'll have me.'

For an answer, she reached out and caught his face between her hands, her eyes large and luminous in the dark.

'You're smug, and you're arrogant, and you're a bit of a prat.'

'And a true bastard.' He nodded. 'Don't forget that one.'

'No, that one I won't allow,' she said, her voice shaking, 'but I love you, too, Elijah Munroe. Even when you called me silly, and stupid, and a doormat—'

'I didn't mean that,' he said, alarm appearing in his eyes. 'I was angry, just lashing out—'

'I know you were,' she said softly. 'Don't forget I've called you some pretty rough things when I was angry.'

'I just…' His voice broke. 'I don't want you to leave me, Brontë.'

She could see the shadows of his past in his eyes, and

vowed that, even if it took her a lifetime, she was somehow going to erase them.

'Eli, I'm always going to love you even when you're crotchety, even when you get right up my nose, and even when we argue as we're bound to,' she said, her voice trembling slightly. 'I am never, *ever* going to stop loving you, and I am never going to leave you.'

And to prove it, she tilted her head, and kissed him, giving him everything she had, holding nothing back, feeling his familiar heat, his strength, as he wrapped his arms around her to kiss her back, and this time it was even better than before because this time she knew it was for keeps, and they would be together, always.

'So is that a yes, you'll marry me?' he said breathlessly into her hair when they had to draw apart to breathe.

'What do you think?' She chuckled.

'I want to hear you say it,' he insisted. 'I want you to say, "Elijah Munroe, I love you and I'll marry you as soon as we can."'

'Kiss me again, and then I'll give you an answer,' she replied, unable to prevent herself from teasing him just a little.

And he did kiss her again. Kissed her until she had to clutch onto his shirt, feeling breathless and giddy, so when their MDT bleeped insistently she groaned against Eli's mouth.

'I told them we were off the road,' she protested. 'I told them the ambulance had broken down and we couldn't take any calls.'

Eli glanced down at the screen, then his lips quirked.

'I think you'd better read what it says,' he declared.

'Why?' she said in confusion, and, when his smile widened she gazed down at the MDT, then across at him in confusion.

There, across the screen, were the words, 'We can't stand the suspense. Are you going to marry him, or not?'

'What the…? How can they…? How do they…?' She faltered, and then her cheeks flushed scarlet and she frantically stretched across the dashboard, and switched off the radio receiver. 'Oh, criminy, Eli, did you realise the radio was still on?'

He shook his head.

'You must have left it on by mistake when you patched EMDC to tell them our ambulance was out of commission,' he replied, reaching for her again only to see her put up her hands to fend him off.

'But that means everyone heard what you said, and everyone heard what I said,' she wailed. 'They were all *listening*, Eli.'

'I don't give a damn.'

'I do,' she protested. 'Oh, this is so embarrassing. Can't you see how embarrassing this is?'

'Only if you tell me you don't want to marry me.'

'But we're never going to live it down,' she declared, putting her hands to her hot cheeks. 'We must have sounded… Those kisses, do you think they heard those kisses?'

'I doubt they heard them.' He laughed. 'But I should imagine they managed to put two and two together during the long silences when we weren't talking, plus there was all that heavy breathing, of course.'

'It isn't *funny*, Eli,' she exclaimed, and he caught both of her hands in his tightly.

'Brontë, everyone heard me tell you I loved you. Everyone heard me ask you to marry me, so look on the bright side. I can't back out now even if I wanted to. Not if I don't want to be lynched.'

She stared up into his deep blue eyes uncertainly. 'And do you—want to back out?'

'Not now, not ever, so quit with the stalling, O'Brian. Will you marry me?'

There was love, and tenderness, and a great deal of

uncertainty, in his face, and it was that uncertainty which tugged at her heart, and brought a tremulous smile to her lips.

'Of course I will, you idiot.'

And she leant towards him to kiss him again, but he put a hand out to stay her.

'Just one minute,' he said firmly, though his eyes, she noticed, were gleaming, and he leant forward and switched on the radio receiver again. 'I don't want you to be able to back out of this either, so, in front of witnesses, Brontë O'Brian, will you marry me?'

'Yes, Elijah Munroe, I will,' she said, and saw him switch off the receiver again. 'So, it's official now, neither of us can back out.'

'Nope. We're stuck with each other,' he replied, and then the corners of his mouth tipped up ever so slightly. 'So, what now?'

'What do you mean, what now?' she asked, and saw his smile widen.

'Well, we're stuck in this ambulance with nothing to do until the breakdown truck arrives.'

'We can listen to the radio,' she suggested. 'Earwig on other paramedics.'

'Nope, that's not lighting my fire.'

'Or we could play I Spy,' she observed. 'I can think of some pretty fiendish ones.'

'I can think of better games to play,' he said, sliding his arm along her seat, and she shook her head.

'I'm sure you can, but we're not playing any of those, not in an ambulance.'

He stuck out his tongue at her. 'Spoilsport.'

'Realist, more like.' She grinned. 'I'm already notorious on the radio, and I've no intention of becoming even more so should the breakdown truck arrive.'

'We could just abandon the ambulance, go back to your place?'

She shook her head at him.

'Eli Munroe, you're a very dangerous man.'

He laughed. 'Nah. Big pussycat, me. So what do you say—will we go back to your place? I mean, we could be sitting here all night, getting colder, and colder, and you have a lovely, warm and very cosy bed....'

It sounded so tempting, and his eyes were hot, and as he'd said, they had no idea when the breakdown truck would arrive. In fact, when she'd told Dispatch of the problem with the ambulance, the caller had been anything but encouraging.

'Okay, we'll get a taxi back to my place,' she said, but as she made to open her door, Eli stayed her arm.

'Just one question before we go,' he declared. 'Do you have a tape measure at home?'

'I...I think so,' she said, bewildered. 'In fact, I'm almost positive I do. Why?'

'Because there's one question you still haven't given me the answer to.' He grinned. 'So, in about half an hour's time, when I've got you naked in front of me...'

'Are you naked in this scene, too?' she said, her lips curving.

'Oh, absolutely.' He nodded. 'Most definitely.'

'So, when I'm naked, and you're naked?' she prompted.

'With your tape measure, I'll finally get to find out what your hip measurement is.'

'I promise you the results will be ugly.' She smiled. 'In fact, it might make you reconsider your offer to marry me.'

He lifted her hand to his lips, his blue eyes soft, and warm.

'Even if you turn out to have hips the size of a barn door—'

'*Hey!*'

'Nothing is going to stop me from marrying you, Brontë O'Brian. We're a partnership now in every sense of the word, and we always will be.'

And as she gazed back at him, and saw the love in his eyes, she knew they would be.

MILLS & BOON

SEPTEMBER 2010 HARDBACK TITLES

ROMANCE

A Stormy Greek Marriage	Lynne Graham
Unworldly Secretary, Untamed Greek	Kim Lawrence
The Sabbides Secret Baby	Jacqueline Baird
The Undoing of de Luca	Kate Hewitt
Katrakis's Last Mistress	Caitlin Crews
Surrender to Her Spanish Husband	Maggie Cox
Passion, Purity and the Prince	Annie West
For Revenge or Redemption?	Elizabeth Power
Red Wine and Her Sexy Ex	Kate Hardy
Every Girl's Secret Fantasy	Robyn Grady
Cattle Baron Needs a Bride	Margaret Way
Passionate Chef, Ice Queen Boss	Jennie Adams
Sparks Fly with Mr Mayor	Teresa Carpenter
Rescued in a Wedding Dress	Cara Colter
Wedding Date with the Best Man	Melissa McClone
Maid for the Single Dad	Susan Meier
Alessandro and the Cheery Nanny	Amy Andrews
Valentino's Pregnancy Bombshell	Amy Andrews

HISTORICAL

Reawakening Miss Calverley	Sylvia Andrew
The Unmasking of a Lady	Emily May
Captured by the Warrior	Meriel Fuller

MEDICAL™

Dating the Millionaire Doctor	Marion Lennox
A Knight for Nurse Hart	Laura Iding
A Nurse to Tame the Playboy	Maggie Kingsley
Village Midwife, Blushing Bride	Gill Sanderson

SEPTEMBER 2010 LARGE PRINT TITLES

ROMANCE

Virgin on Her Wedding Night	Lynne Graham
Blackwolf's Redemption	Sandra Marton
The Shy Bride	Lucy Monroe
Penniless and Purchased	Julia James
Beauty and the Reclusive Prince	Raye Morgan
Executive: Expecting Tiny Twins	Barbara Hannay
A Wedding at Leopard Tree Lodge	Liz Fielding
Three Times A Bridesmaid...	Nicola Marsh

HISTORICAL

The Viscount's Unconventional Bride	Mary Nichols
Compromising Miss Milton	Michelle Styles
Forbidden Lady	Anne Herries

MEDICAL™

The Doctor's Lost-and-Found Bride	Kate Hardy
Miracle: Marriage Reunited	Anne Fraser
A Mother for Matilda	Amy Andrews
The Boss and Nurse Albright	Lynne Marshall
New Surgeon at Ashvale A&E	Joanna Neil
Desert King, Doctor Daddy	Meredith Webber

0910 Gen Std HB

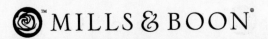

OCTOBER 2010 HARDBACK TITLES

ROMANCE

The Reluctant Surrender	Penny Jordan
Shameful Secret, Shotgun Wedding	Sharon Kendrick
The Virgin's Choice	Jennie Lucas
Scandal: Unclaimed Love-Child	Melanie Milburne
Powerful Greek, Housekeeper Wife	Robyn Donald
Hired by Her Husband	Anne McAllister
Snowbound Seduction	Helen Brooks
A Mistake, A Prince and A Pregnancy	Maisey Yates
Champagne with a Celebrity	Kate Hardy
When He was Bad…	Anne Oliver
Accidentally Pregnant!	Rebecca Winters
Star-Crossed Sweethearts	Jackie Braun
A Miracle for His Secret Son	Barbara Hannay
Proud Rancher, Precious Bundle	Donna Alward
Cowgirl Makes Three	Myrna Mackenzie
Secret Prince, Instant Daddy!	Raye Morgan
Officer, Surgeon…Gentleman!	Janice Lynn
Midwife in the Family Way	Fiona McArthur

HISTORICAL

Innocent Courtesan to Adventurer's Bride	Louise Allen
Disgrace and Desire	Sarah Mallory
The Viking's Captive Princess	Michelle Styles

MEDICAL™

Bachelor of the Baby Ward	Meredith Webber
Fairytale on the Children's Ward	Meredith Webber
Playboy Under the Mistletoe	Joanna Neil
Their Marriage Miracle	Sue MacKay

0910 Gen Std LP

MILLS & BOON

ROMANCE

Marriage: To Claim His Twins	Penny Jordan
The Royal Baby Revelation	Sharon Kendrick
Under the Spaniard's Lock and Key	Kim Lawrence
Sweet Surrender with the Millionaire	Helen Brooks
Miracle for the Girl Next Door	Rebecca Winters
Mother of the Bride	Caroline Anderson
What's A Housekeeper To Do?	Jennie Adams
Tipping the Waitress with Diamonds	Nina Harrington

HISTORICAL

Practical Widow to Passionate Mistress	Louise Allen
Major Westhaven's Unwilling Ward	Emily Bascom
Her Banished Lord	Carol Townend

MEDICAL™

The Nurse's Brooding Boss	Laura Iding
Emergency Doctor and Cinderella	Melanie Milburne
City Surgeon, Small Town Miracle	Marion Lennox
Bachelor Dad, Girl Next Door	Sharon Archer
A Baby for the Flying Doctor	Lucy Clark
Nurse, Nanny...Bride!	Alison Roberts